A Dream Within A Dream

Gregory L. Norris

Book Clubs & Special Ordering:

Quantity sales. Special discounts are available on quantity purchases by **book clubs,** corporations, associations, and others. For details, contact the publisher at director@vanvelzerpress.com.

Cover design by Trisha Lewis

Edits & Layout & Publishing via Van Velzer Press
Paperback ISBN: 9 7 8 - 1 - 9 5 4 2 5 3 - 2 0 - 9
Hardback ISBN: 9 7 8 - 1 - 9 5 4 2 5 3 - 2 2 - 3
Ebook ISBN: 9 7 8 - 1 - 9 5 4 2 5 3 - 2 3 - 0

LCCN Available upon request
director@vanvelzerpress.com

Printed in the United States of America

TABLE OF CONTENTS

A DREAM WITHIN A DREAM

LEN

She moved to fix his tie. He turned away, catching a look at his reflection in the standing oval mirror of the unfamiliar bedroom where most of the little they owned was still in boxes and, for a moment, he was only half there, more ghost than man.

"Come on. We don't want to be late," she said, and how distant her voice sounded, as though beckoning from a different life, the one the ghost knew before he died.

"Late," Joe Devere repeated in a voice sounding even farther away.

* * *

His Winston cigarette burned in the Mustang's ashtray mostly unsmoked. Like everything else in this world, the act of smoking had lost its pleasure, its coolness; he only went through the motion as a way to keep busy, keep moving, alive, when he worried and believed he was already dead. He'd died overseas in that place, only his body still functioned and wasn't yet aware that it had expired.

They traveled down part of a road where the towering oaks formed a kind of living cathedral and into a stretch of darkness, the sun still visible around the edges. For a terrible moment, the Mustang became a Jeep, the roadside dense jungle, and he wasn't with his wife but fellow soldiers unlucky enough to have won a lottery no young American male aged eighteen to twenty-five wanted to claim. The last of the summer's warmth streaming in through open windows doubled its heat. Joe gripped the wheel. The world ahead of him blurred.

She spoke his name. He blinked. The nightmare jungle superimposed over their surroundings faded, though not fully; it, too, a ghost that haunted him wherever he turned. Joe realized he was holding his breath, the last sip of air bottled inside his lungs now volcanic. He exhaled.

"You okay?"

"Yeah, fine," he lied.

They drove on.

* * *

Hubert Weller's place was a big stone palace not quite as impressive as the campus of Hollings Head College, but close enough—proof of tenure, at least. Joe parked the 'stang in a circular drive marked at both ends by gray granite obelisks. She waited for him to open her car door. He did. They went through the visuals of happiness for show.

On the walk along the flagstone path to the garden, he caught the sweet fragrance of mowed lawn and tried to remember that it had once been one of his favorite smells. But the green now filled him with something other ... a reminder of swamps and raw nerves and unholy humidity and bloodshed and—

Laughter rose from the courtyard where professors and their wives carried on naive social lives, obliviously ignorant to the war being fought on the other side of the world far from their small Rhode Island sovereignty. At quick glance, none of the cocktail reception's guests looked to be younger than a hundred. The wives were all pearls and matronly hairstyles, the husbands codgers who smoked expensive brands of cigarettes and drank the finest scotch. They lived and breathed their work as gods of the all-male studentry.

That thought left Joe jealous—not for their tenure but that they lived and breathed.

"Aah, it's our newest adjunct," Weller addressed the couple with theatrical flourish.

All eyes trained upon the newcomers. Joe flashed a smile because that's what was expected.

A DREAM WITHIN A DREAM

"Devere—and Mrs. Devere, I presume," Weller said. "Everyone, meet Hollings Head's new music instructor and his lovely wife ... ?"

"Gia," she said.

Mrs. Weller approached. "How lovely—and unusual!"

"It's short for Ligeia," she said, taking much of the attention off his shoulders, for which he was grateful.

Drinks were offered. Joe scored a scotch. It was as exquisite as he imagined yet offered zero pleasure.

"You've got your work cut out for you, Devere," Weller said after the sun set and the party moved inside to a large drawing room past the two sets of French doors. "Bunch of spoiled rich brats expecting to get out of the draft pool based upon family name and privilege."

"I'll do my best," Joe said.

The room was part library, with shelves along one wall mostly filled with old hardcovers, and part conservatory, according to the piano and selection of musical instruments, a harp among them.

"Oh, you must play for us!" Mrs. Weller said. "I hear you're quite the musician."

"I used to be," Joe said and punctuated the answer with a nervous chuckle that sounded lunatic even to his ears. "That was a long time ago."

Four years, his inner voice reminded after doing the math. *Before the war. Before you died.*

"Oh, come on, Devere," Weller pressed. "Play something."

Joe glanced over. Weller held an M16 assault rifle in bloodied hands. Joe's next breath hitched in his throat. He blinked, and the rifle was a guitar.

"I don't really do that anymore," the apparition in control of his voice said separately from the sudden ice cracking over the rest of his anatomy.

He thawed enough to make it over to the piano, where he played *Clair de Lune* and *Für Elise*—safe, sweet offerings meant to charm and not offend. Devere was the new guy; the guy who would be expected going forward to perform every time he gathered with the real teachers for their displays of power and hierarchy.

* * *

She reached for him.

He turned away and faced the wall.

Not long after, the cadence of her breaths told him the martinis had worked their magic and, if the Fates were kinder to her than him on this night, she would sleep without dreams.

He slipped from their bed and navigated by the light of the moon through the boxes to the bathroom. Their small rented cottage was nowhere near as audacious as Hubert Keller's manor, but it felt twice as cavernous without furniture, offering only an emptiness that turned the soft scuffle of his bare soles across the ancient hardwood floor into an echo. In the kitchen, he lit a cigarette but soon stubbed it out in the heavy glass ashtray where other barely-smoked butts sat in broken piles. He ran the cold water and splashed his face. Then, looking up, he again caught his reflection, now in the window glass, his flesh embossed in moonlight.

He wore his dark hair neat except where his styling cream failed in its perpetual tug of war against that one cowlick. A prickle of five o'clock scruff coated his chin, cheeks, and throat at just after midnight. His eyes weren't merely green but the color of emerald gemstones.

Joe stepped back and, in turning, caught his full reflection in the glass of the kitchen door. His body, clad only in boxers, was athletic, a soldier's. A T-pattern of dark hair covered his bare chest. More coated his legs. His abdomen was a washboard of muscle. Handsome, he supposed, but it was difficult to be sure because a cloud chose that moment to pass in front of the moon, and the room dimmed. His image vanished into shadows.

Besides, what does it matter? Handsome wouldn't have protected me any more than it had Stokely or Rodriguez. They were attractive, young men, too, and they're dead.

Not for the first time, he wondered if the same held true for Joe Devere.

* * *

A DREAM WITHIN A DREAM

On that morning, he sipped coffee, which tasted bitter, ate half a slice of toast, and dressed in his black suit and trousers, black wingtips, white button-down shirt, and thin black tie.

"A stylish, modern man of 1965," she said as he picked up his worn leather satchel and headed out the door without pecking a kiss to her cheek.

The morning dawned foggy and gray, a dubious gift from the nearby Atlantic. He drove with the window open. The saline air tried to distract him with thoughts of lazy beach days from a youth long over. His nerves crackled, but he couldn't tell if it was the new pressure of the first day at Hollings Head College or something older and cancerous devouring him from the inside, a ravenous malignancy picked up overseas lodged in the soft lining of his gut, feasting on what remained of his corpse.

Then he heard the bells carry through the mist, a carillon that, somehow, lightened his burden and seemed to guide him forward. As their tintinnabulation drifted in the air, he caught sight of the indestructible towers and halls of this college for young men.

The bells—ringing from the famous Music Hall.

Joe tipped a glance at its square, gray stone spire and almost, almost smiled.

* * *

He set his satchel on top of the acre of wooden desk, a bridgehead between he and his students. While writing his name on the chalkboard, they filed into the classroom. From a side cut of his eye, he recorded the parade, all of its participants clad in khaki slacks, white button-downs, navy blazers, and ties.

Uniforms, Joe thought and regretted the quip.

Uniforms.

Turning, he swept the room with a glance and wondered how many of the young men would be drafted as soldiers, go far away, and return in body bags.

"I'm Mister Devere," the voice acting separately from the rest of his consciousness announced. "Welcome to Music Theory..."

* * *

He half smoked another Winston, aware that the ashy taste had refueled his nausea. On the walk in from the teacher's private patio, the sun broke through the clouds, and the day not only brightened from its moody black and white palette but also warmed.

Joe marched down the long hallway and did his best to not go there again. Marching. Through chest-deep water. Struggling to breathe. Marching. And there were things in that water. Marching—

A distant melody teased his ear, beautiful, elegiac, from a piano. As he neared his classroom, he realized the music originated from behind the door, now ajar, and the relic of the upright wedged into the corner at the back of the space that was his to command.

Like a barely remembered dream, he nearly identified the composition. *One of the classics? No*—he guessed it was new. *Something on the radio.* At the door, he identified it—a piano version of *Mister Dieingly Sad* by the Critters.

He pushed the door open. A figure sat at the piano, back turned toward him. By the clothes, Joe assumed the bold musician was one of his students. The music crescendoed, and the performance seamlessly transitioned to another lamentation, this one Joe remembered clearly—Chad and Jeremy's *Willow Weep for Me*.

The melody played out with precision. More so, it was beautiful. So much so that, at first, Joe overlooked the musician's other details—blond hair in a golden mop, willowy body, and, though he couldn't see them, he heard the confidence in those fingers as they glided over the keys and drove out most of the gloom that had pursued Joe into the classroom.

He listened, struggling for breaths that refused to come easily.

The music cut out.

The musician turned, alerted to his audience of one by the clearing of Joe's throat.

Time froze.

Joe swallowed, and the clock resumed moving.

Young, attractive—no, *stunning,* Joe thought. Angelic, the young man studied him in return and smiled. Joe sensed all of the emotion drain from his expression.

"Sorry, couldn't help myself," the young man said. "Too excited."

A DREAM WITHIN A DREAM

"Excited?" Joe parroted.

"Sure, the music."

"Music?"

The musician swept a short sequence across the keys. The melody resonated for another glorious second. "The music."

Their glances connected, and Joe wondered if he was still dreaming—or if he'd died and the heavens had sent him an angel to guide him into his afterlife. Joe loosened his tie. Their gazes remained locked—Joe's emerald greens and the angel's summer blues.

"Did you like it?" the young man asked.

"Huh?"

"The music?"

Joe nodded and choked down another dry swallow. "Yeah."

The confession widened the smile on the musician's face, enough to reveal a length of clean white teeth.

From behind them, more bodies streamed in. The musician jumped up from the piano bench, grabbed the book bag near his feet, and scooted up to one of the seats at the head of the row of student desks.

Joe unstuck and returned to the barrier of his bridgehead. He willed his consciousness to compose itself and ran through the introduction protocol for the fourth time that morning.

"I'm Mister Devere, and welcome to Music Theory," he said, aware of the young man's study from the front row. "It is my hope that you'll leave here with a solid appreciation for the history and future of this particular art." He pulled out the attendance sheet and ran down the list of a dozen names. "Allen, James?"

"Here," one of the students in the middle row answered.

Three names later, Joe asked, "Crawford, Len?"

The angel raised his hand and said, "Here, Mister Devere."

Joe glanced up from his sheet. The angel's smile was on full display, his hand with its long, elegant fingers tempting his focus to linger. Joe caught himself staring and forced his eyes back to the sheet and continued.

"Peck, Avimos," he read the last name on the list.

"Present," grunted a deep voice from the back row.

Joe looked. Avimos Peck, unlike Len Crawford, was a muscular athlete with a brush-cut, likely one of Hollings Head's star football players and, no doubt, a privileged silver spoon of the type Hubert Weller had warned of judging by the young man's tone.

He noticed Len Crawford's hand was still up.

Joe nodded.

The musician's hand lowered. "When can we play?"

"Play?"

"The music."

Joe chuckled, and how good it felt, how sane it sounded.

"Homo," a voice from the back of the class huffed.

Joe narrowed his gaze and shot a look past the musician to the same young athlete, now chewing on the end of his pencil. "Something you wish to share with the rest of the class, Mister Peck?"

"No," Avimos Peck said.

"No what?"

"No, sir," the offender said.

Joe's glare lingered until the Peck boy diverted his gaze, indicating he surrendered first.

Another quick glimpse of Len Crawford showed he was still smiling, still radiant. An unfamiliar lightness filled Joe. Only after the bell rang and his fourth period students filtered out of the classroom did he understand it for what it was: the first happiness he'd known for a long, long while.

* * *

She sat at the kitchen table, one of the long, slim cigarettes designed specifically for the hands of lady smokers clutched between pointer and middle fingers. A casserole baked in the oven.

"How was it?" Gia asked.

He shrugged. "You know, work."

A DREAM WITHIN A DREAM

He kissed the top of her head, more ceremony. "I need a shower."

In the bedroom, he stripped out of his suit and shirt, peeled off his socks and boxers, then padded into the bathroom. He stepped under the hot spray and closed his eyes. Len Crawford's face surfaced in his mind's camera along with the magical music. Joe masturbated, aware of the smile no one saw, and when he climaxed, the cascade washed away his guilt.

* * *

He dressed in jeans, a sweater over a clean white undershirt, and old sneakers—relics from that foggy time before the war when he unofficially died.

She served dinner.

He ate, clutching the fork less like a college professor and more like a caveman. She didn't comment on that point. The food had no taste.

A cool breeze gossiped through the new dusk. He smoked outside and gazed up at a waning moon. The first crisp note of autumn carried on the wind's billows. Joe attempted to remember boyhood Halloweens and colored leaves ironed between sheets of wax paper. Failing that, he recalled Len.

"The music," Joe whispered.

The wind carried the words past his ears on the cigarette smoke and scattered them in the darkness.

* * *

She touched him, her desire telegraphed without words.

All the moisture drained from his mouth. He worked free of his boxers. Details blurred. He entered her. But like all else in the world, the sensation had become gray and two-dimensional. Her soft mewls beneath him restored thoughts about the baby that never was real, lost in tears and blood soon after conception before his deployment. The memory escaped past his mental revetments for all of a second before he wrangled it back under control. And then his wife wasn't his wife but Len Crawford.

That moment conjured more than his orgasm, which rose in a surge of heat and light so intense in its unexpectedness that he howled. Shudders wracked his flesh, even the ice fiery.

He jumped off her and hastened into the bathroom. There, he bent over the toilet and vomited.

* * *

Joe entered the classroom wearing the mask he showed the rest of the world fixed in place and more invisible barriers constructed in his mind. Even so, his pulse quickened as the morning wore on and students arrived then departed.

The clock slowed. Time distorted.

Joe turned away from the wall where the clock was a blur and nudged up his suit coat's sleeve. His watch was also paralyzed.

He heard singing from somewhere just outside the door, and the rest of time stuck apart from that one detail. Len entered the room and seemed to bring that unique bent of the September sunlight in with him.

"Mister Devere," he said, and oh—how Joe could get used to the way this young man spoke his name, as though invoking the most important part of a magic spell.

He maintained his façade even as his insides dissolved and offered a nod in greeting. The young man again took his seat at the front of the class. Secretly, Joe watched Len Crawford sit. Even that small act was filled with energy and effervescence. It was as though every move the young man made was celebratory.

"How are you today, Crawford?" Joe asked, all business.

"*Wunderbah*," Len answered.

That one, unexpected word, spoken with such passion, shattered the veneer erected over his vulnerability. Unable to trap it, his smile was back, wide and unapologetic—on full display as the other students filed in and took their seats. He sweated. Getting past the invisible defenses that formed boundaries and borders, Joe opened the closest of the room's four windows. Warm September air rich with the fragrance of mowed grass and sunlight and a trace of the ocean near Sugar Beach swept in.

"Mister Devere?" Len called at his back.

Joe hesitated, barely kept from turning around. "Yes, Crawford?" he asked over his shoulder.

"The Music Hall."

"What about it?"

"I've read that it was designed to utilize perfect pitch. That Franz Liszt and Felix Mendelssohn performed there."

"About a million years ago," Peck huffed around an unpleasant, idiotic chuckle. "Queer," he added beneath his breath.

Joe straightened and faced the young man at the back of the room, sudden rage filling his belly with hot coals lit by words. "Mister Peck, is there a problem?"

Peck snickered again and leaned back in his seat as far as the chair allowed. "No problem, sir."

"Because twice now I swear I've heard you utter the kind of talk that has no place in my classroom. Certainly not in an institution of higher learning like Hollings Head College."

Peck smirked. "I did not, Mister Devere."

Joe's focus on Peck lingered. "Are you suggesting there's a problem with my hearing?"

"No, sir."

"Good. Make sure I don't hear it again."

He strode back to the head of the class and had them take out their books. Then he inched his gaze once more to the magnificent creature in the front row.

"And to answer your question, Crawford, yes—they and other notables have performed here. Before you ask, as music professor, yes, I have a key to the Music Hall and I'll see what I can do about making either a formal—or informal—visit there for the class happen."

Len's smile returned, and how it filled Joe with sunshine knowing he'd contributed to the young man's *joie de vivre.*

At the end of that class, they handed in papers. Joe gathered them up and tucked them into the leather slipcase in his satchel for grading.

* * *

She retired early after dinner.

He sat in the living room with a cold beer and work. Grading papers allowed him to vanish from his surroundings. Most of it was as flat and banal as he expected. He reached the fourth period students' pile, and his heart resumed its gallop.

"Len," Joe whispered.

There was the young musician's homework, written in elegant cursive, the penmanship a celebration, the page and its words filled with primal energy. Unable to resist, Joe brought it to his face and inhaled the imaginary scent of Len Crawford. As he did, he noticed something—what turned out being a second sheet stuck to the first, perhaps ripped from his student's writing tablet at the same time as the homework assignment.

He peeled the sheets apart.

And read what was written on the second.

A DREAM WITHIN A DREAM

HYMN
Desiderium cordis mei
Audi orationem meam, superi

> He walked into that crowded room
> But all I saw was him.
> Was I only dreaming?
> He, only mist, a whim?
>
> A ghost to haunt with desire
> Our eyes made love.
> And then the fire.
> Don't wake up!
>
> I sing this song in silence
> Praying for an alliance.
> A hymn
> To him.

Desiderium cordis mei
Audi orationem meam, superi

A poem? No, the lyrics to a song.

How long he stared, reading and rereading, Joe couldn't tell. But the night had advanced, and the smile was back on his face. A song. One filled with mystery and sensuality.

A song written about me, he thought.

Electricity tingled over and under his flesh, teasing epidermis, blood, and marrow. Deeper even—to that place he used to believe was soul. When Joe stood to stretch, he found himself erect. He read the song once more and hummed the lyrics to something his earlier self, that former music maker, created on the spot. He didn't know Latin. The song reached its end, and he realized it would never be sung the same way again because the melody had dissolved within the cottage's walls.

* * *

He approached Hubert Weller in the teacher's lounge and pulled the slip he'd jotted the words on from his coat's pocket. "Can you translate something for me?" Joe asked. "It's Latin."

Weller ran an eye over the scrawl. "*Desiderium cordis mei*—my heart's desire."

"And the rest?"

"*Audi orationem meam, superi* means, hear my plea, gods," Weller said. "Is this part of some song you're teaching your students, Devere?"

Joe absorbed the meaning behind the translation. "Something like that." He thanked Weller, took back the words from a dead and powerful language, and wandered down the long hallway in a kind of daze, his steps feeling lighter than before the war, no longer so sure he'd died.

* * *

Joe inched his focus around to the first row. The young man's smile was there, always there, like a counterpoint to challenge his perpetual scowl.

Joe moved along the aisles between desks, placing each student's paper before him. It was his pleasure to hand an A to Len Crawford.

A DREAM WITHIN A DREAM

"Well done. You've earned extra points for the latter, Mister Crawford."

Len looked up, his smile still present but now within it a look of bewilderment. As Joe returned to the invisible line he'd drawn in the sand of the classroom's molecules, he watched Len scramble through his writing tablet. With the page gone, Len turned over his homework and saw the missing lyrics along with Joe's small note: *Great Work*, unsigned.

Red rose up Len's throat to color his cheeks, and Joe did his best to not think of that embarrassed flesh blossoming for other reasons.

"You can all take a page from Mister Crawford's outstanding example," he said without making eye contact. "Now, if you'd all open your books to chapter three..."

* * *

Too soon, fourth period ended and students hastened out of his classroom. The first to arrive was, no surprise, the last to exit. "Mister Crawford, a word," Joe called after the young man, who looked to be in no rush to depart.

Suddenly, Len Crawford was on the other side of his desk, and the full scope of his beauty threatened to punch Joe with the force of a physical blow.

"Yes, Mister Devere?"

Joe sucked in a cleansing breath and opened the desk's center drawer. The key to the Music Hall was hidden beneath various ephemera, secured to a black velvet ribbon. Joe produced the key. "I thought you might want to visit the Music Hall some time. Maybe help me with the season's upcoming concert schedule?"

Len's smile widened. To Joe, the young man appeared equally as ready to collapse in the strange but undeniable chemical spark that flickered between them.

"Really?" Len gasped.

Joe projected confidence. "Sure. I'd appreciate the assist. And..."

"And?"

Getting the words past his lips required more effort than he'd expected. "You're really talented. You have a gift."

Len's embarrassment crept back. He flashed a nervous grin. "I didn't mean to—" The sentence went unfinished, and though he didn't think it possible, Joe found the young man even more charming as a result of his awkwardness.

"It's beautiful," Joe said, his voice not much louder than a whisper.

Len turned away. "It's nothing. Just something that came to me in a dream."

"A dream?"

"I dream in music," Len clarified. "It's like a dream within a dream. But I also eat music. Breathe it. Live it. Sometimes, it's so overwhelming I want to cry. Do you ever feel that way, Mister Devere? That the beauty of music—and even its ugliness—is so pure, so everything, that you want to cry, and you do?"

Joe laughed, though not in dismissal. "I haven't cried since…" Now it was his turn to leave thoughts incomplete, declarations hanging over precipices, truths unrevealed. A curious silence settled between them, one in which words weren't necessary, only the bottled glances they both cast over the barrier of Joe's desk.

"When?" Len whispered.

"The Music Hall?" Joe smiled and swung the key on its black velvet ribbon around his pointer finger.

* * *

He wandered past the courtyard, aware of the warm, gray breeze, the last of the summer's green smell, and also of his breathless anticipation. The first colored leaves showed overhead—maples, most in pale yellows, a few displaying the deep red of fresh blood.

The walking path turned toward a row of granite benches where students and sometimes staff wandered to ponder life's conundrums. The biggest mystery in Joe's new life sat in a jaunty pose with two pencils-turned-drumsticks and beat a sweet sound onto the makeshift drum set of the stone bench between his spread legs.

In that moment before their gazes again connected, Joe drank in Len's image. The young man had loosened his tie. His blue eyes radiated energy—with the pure, cosmic spark of the universe.

A DREAM WITHIN A DREAM

Joe wondered if he'd ever experienced a fraction of that level of happiness. Then he realized he was living it in that very instant.

"Mister Devere," Len said.

Again, Joe considered what it would be like to hear his name whispered, moaned, from those lips, that smile which begged to be kissed. "Ready?" he asked, his mouth suddenly as arid as the desert.

Len stowed his drumsticks in his book bag, jumped off the bench, and bounded over to Joe. The young man's movements stirred the fragrance of the royal purple asters growing in wild tangles along the walking path and something more—a hint of clean sweat mixed with subtle cologne.

The scent of Len.

Joe surrendered more of himself on the final walk to the Music Hall. The tall gray cathedral was alone in a corner of the campus. Its gravel parking lot empty, no one else out to wander the walking paths as the sky roiled with threatening rain clouds, it was only the two of them.

Joe pulled the key out of his suit coat pocket on his way up the stone steps to the imposing double doors. An inner voice of reason attempted to remind him of facts associated with the structure in those final few sane seconds before the lock released: constructed in early 1820 to house the pipe organ, biggest in the country at the time, the envy of New York, Boston, and Philadelphia, it had put Hollings Head, Rhode Island, on the map. Now their surroundings seemed part of a reality that existed free of the rest of the world.

The doors opened. The smell of lemon polish and museums drifted out past the threshold. Even without switching on the massive candelabra-style chandeliers, the enormous stained glass windows of the main spire lit the Music Hall in a dazzling kaleidoscope of cobalt blue, forest green, ruby red, and amethyst fractals.

Len entered, eyes wide, looking as though he'd experienced some form of religious awakening. He meandered into the main hall, through its varnished wooden rows of benches to stand in front of the stage, where the pipes of the organ rose skyward among colonnades of exquisite carvings of cherubs, rosettes, and wedding cake molding ... up, up, toward those Heaven-facing windows.

Joe pursued him into the heart of the space. Even the scuffle his soles made across the marble floor sounded musical, the pitch perfect.

Len smiled. The rest of his expression appeared on the verge of tears.

Joe smiled too. "What do you think?" His question floated over their heads and resonated like a baritone melody.

"I think..." Len began.

And then he tossed his arms around Joe and hugged him.

Joe froze. So close, the young man's body fell under the shadow of his height and physique and looked so small, so elegant, so attractive. Joe detected more of Len's scent in their unexpected closeness, and it intoxicated him.

"Thank you, Mister Devere," Len whispered, his voice bewitching and warm against Joe's knotted throat.

Joe patted the young man's shoulder when he wanted to do more, so much more. To embrace him in return. To taste his mouth. To test the Music Hall's claim about perfect pitch even with the music of gasps and sighs during lovemaking.

Len glanced up, and Joe wanted to cry, too, but he was long past that ability. It was there in Len's eyes, the breathless anticipation that comes before a first kiss.

"I can't," Joe growled. "I want to, but I can't."

"Why?"

"Because I'm really dead and owned by the grave. All here is Limbo, land of lost souls."

Len straightened, slipped his hand under Joe's suit coat, and settled his palm over the patch of white button-down and undershirt atop Joe's heart, the act curiously more intimate than the many Joe had fantasized throughout the past week.

"Lub-dub, lub-dub," Len said. His voice carried around them to echo off the tiny wings, feet, and vacant stares of the hundred carved cherubs witnessing their forbidden closeness. "I can hear your heartbeat," Len continued. "You're still alive, Mister Devere."

"I am?" Joe asked in a voice almost not there.

Len smiled and nodded.

Joe seized hold of the young man's wrist, drew Len's hand off his heart, and crushed their mouths together. Len moaned while Joe inhaled his surrender. He held on. Len melted beneath him. The Music Hall resonated as the first of the storm's rain pelted its tall windows. The world turned in its orbit, and Joe Devere took one large step back from the edge of the grave.

* * *

They got soaked on the jog back to the staff parking lot where Joe's 'stang waited alone as early dusk hurried in with the rain storm.

Joe unlocked the door, got in, and opened the passenger's side. Len scooted in beside him. The rain beat a primal melody on the hardtop's roof. The car bottled the clean smell of the rain mixed with their sweat.

"You live on campus?" Joe asked.

"Buxton Hall," Len answered.

Joe studied the young man in the brewing darkness. "I'll drive you."

"No, I love the rain. I'll walk," Len said, and Joe believed him. Everything was an experience to be savored, to be sung about, to Len Crawford.

He reached over and caressed his thumb across Len's cheek. Len leaned into Joe's big hand and sighed.

"This can't happen again," Joe said, knowing it was a lie even as he spoke the words. It was no more of a barrier than what he'd attempted to create between his desk and students.

Len kissed his palm, leaned over, and brushed his lips over Joe's. As the young man did this, he reacquainted himself with Joe's stiffness, boldly gripping the tent at the front of his trousers. The kiss ended, too brief, with Len whispering into his ear, "I'm leaving anyway, Mister Devere."

"Joe—my name's Joe."

"Joe..."

There it was, that magical incantation woven from his name. And once spoken, Joe knew he could never live without hearing it invoked with such reverence again by the young man moving away, opening the door, and vanishing into the cascade of tears.

He woke from the spell. "What do you mean—leaving?"

But the door closed, and when Joe looked past the passenger's window, erect and itchy all over, Len Crawford was out of focus and lost in the downpour.

* * *

"You're late," she said.

"Work."

"Dinner's cold. You can heat it up in the oven."

"Okay."

He sat at the table but didn't eat. Wet, his clothes fitting with an unpleasant awkwardness, he stared at his wedding ring and mulled over Len's cryptic words.

* * *

The next morning, he found a sheet of paper on his desk, one run off of a drum printer that still smelled like the wet blue ink. It was decorated in rudimentary drawings of musical instruments and a few clefs.

The Golden Bowl, Joe read. An ad for some music club in town.

He stared down at the handwritten advertisement. Saturday night. Local music. An address. Students entered the classroom. Joe opened the top desk drawer, returned the Music Hall's key, and slid the sheet—the offering from Len—under cover.

* * *

He went through the motions and taught. Outside, a stiff breeze blew and clanked ghost-chains made out of fallen leaves.

Fourth period arrived.

Joe's breath clotted in his throat. He spoke about harmony, rhythm, pitch, meter, and scales. They even attempted their first harmonic exercises which ended with less success than the previous classes. The lone bright spot among a group of twelve taking his course because they had to was Len, who lived for the music.

A DREAM WITHIN A DREAM

Len. Beautiful Len.

The bell rang.

"Mister Crawford, I need to see you," Joe said.

He pulled out his notebook under the guise of making their conference something professional on the surface between teacher and student. Len waited on the far side of Joe's desk, using that demarcation as the other young men shuffled out of the classroom. Not lost on Joe as he reclined in the uncomfortable chair with the hard wooden seat and metal casters that complained of their age was the sour look Avimos Peck cast at both of them.

"The door," Joe said.

Len obeyed the command and closed it. In the time it took for Len to return, Joe realized the young man would do anything he asked, give him anything he wished for. The wind outside the room moaned. The rain had turned the world damp and chilly.

The young man returned to the other side of Joe's desk, his happiness clear. "Will you come tomorrow night?" Before Joe could respond, Len added, "I'm performing."

Joe drank in a breath. On it was Len's scent. "What you said after the Music Hall ... about leaving?"

Len's smile reduced its radiance by half. "I've been thinking about going somewhere else—like New York City. Since the Stonewall Riots ... Somewhere where I can be myself and suffer for my art. Maybe San Francisco."

"Suffer?" Joe asked.

"Sure, isn't that part of the process? To prove to the muses that we're worthy of their gifts? I don't have a lot of money on hand, but some, enough, and my inheritance comes through when I'm twenty-five. Oh, I know what my uncle will do, the wretch, the moment he hears I've dropped out of college. But that gives me seven whole years to make my career work. And by then, if I'm successful, I won't need the fortune my father left me."

At that point, Joe realized Len was regurgitating something jagged he'd swallowed down that needed to be exorcised. He listened.

"Either way, I'll be making music and living my life without having to hide all the time!"

Joe stood. Len's smile had vanished, and all Joe could think about was bringing it back. He rounded the desk and reached for Len, drawing him into the safety of his arms.

"Yes," Joe said.

To the Golden Bowl.

And, both understood, to so much more.

* * *

On that gray Saturday, they ran errands—the dry cleaners, groceries, and the hardware store. Joe hung up pictures where his wife wanted them displayed, and she set out a framed photograph of their wedding on the fireplace mantel in the cottage's living room. He hadn't been much older than Len Crawford on that day, but not lost on him was the spare quality of the smile he offered to the camera.

"I have an engagement tonight," he said after they ate lunch.

"Oh?"

"Work-related." It wasn't so much a lie as an exaggeration of the truth.

"When do we need to leave?"

The sandwich sitting in his gut performed a back flip. "Teachers only this time. It isn't cocktails."

She scowled, and he sensed what would follow. Joe wasn't wrong on that count.

"You've spent so much time there."

"It's my job."

She tsked and stormed away, slamming the bedroom door behind her. Not long after, he heard her sobs, knowing she meant for him to.

* * *

A DREAM WITHIN A DREAM

Hollings Head was a college town and looked it. North Amity Street boasted two bookstores, a stationary and camera shop, art gallery, movie theater, small restaurants, a café, and, at the very end, a tavern painted purple whose basement contained a nightclub and performance space called The Golden Bowl.

Joe circled the parking lot, checked his watch, and let the Mustang idle. Twice, he nearly drove away—back to Gia and the façade of a life that was over almost from the moment it had begun. Guilt tortured him, smothering the combination of hope and happiness attempting to germinate in his gut. He shifted in the driver's seat, unable to face his reflection in the rearview mirror.

Gone to New York or San Francisco, his inner Joe reminded. *Taking that golden smile with him.*

An emotion worse than guilt filled his insides. Exhaling through his mouth, he got out, pocketed his keys, and marched into the purple tavern, conscious of the night's chill and also the giddy sense of anticipation once more in control of his flesh.

The stretch of floor beyond the vestibule led ahead to the upstairs bar and also to the right, down a set of stairs. This part was guarded over by a young man dressed in a smart suit. Joe paid the cover charge from the change in his pockets and strutted down the stairs.

The place wasn't much more than a sad collection of mismatched tables and chairs arranged in a chaotic pattern in front of a stage and microphone. A gaudy cigarette machine greeted music lovers at the base of the stairs. Nicotine-stained walls surrounded all. He fed quarters into the machine and pushed its button. A fresh pack of Winstons with a book of matches dropped down into the tray. Joe caught his reflection in the machine's glass as he lowered to retrieve them—sweater over white undershirt, jeans, unshaved. For the first time, he saw himself as Len did. Time and space warped. He found himself back at the Music Hall, his mouth claiming the young man's. Len's hands gripping him in desperation before one slipped down, touching Joe's maleness. Their moans had shouted hosannas in the highest, the reverberations rising through the spire to charm the angels.

Joe's reflection smiled.

He turned toward the sparse crowd gathered in anticipation of the show and opted for a table in a corner not far from the stage. Feeling more alive than he could recall, he took the seat backwards in that classic pose of cowboys in Westerns and tough guy police dicks in Film Noir, thinking Len would appreciate that. Before the rest of the audience claimed their seats and the lights dimmed, he spun the chair back around and sank down into the shadows.

"Welcome to another night of music on North Amity in our sleepy little town of Hollings Head," an enthusiastic older man dressed in a crimson tuxedo with matching bowtie and cummerbund announced. "It is The Golden Bowl's pleasure to welcome back the haunting stylings of Len Crawford!"

Applause sounded, flat until Joe ramped up the volume, adding a sharp wolf's whistle to enhance the impact. The angel drifted out. Len wore a black turtleneck, beret, blue jeans, and opted for bare feet—heavenly distraction. He carried bongos and took to the chair the crimson man presented. Head bowed at first, he waited—the silence, Joe sensed, intentional. A prelude. And then he played the bongos, the beats short, sharp.

"Lub-dub," Len sang in tune to the drums. "Lub-dub..."

Heartbeats...mine!

The pulse and proof of life continued for half a minute, maybe, in which Joe fell deeper, deeper into the sensory rush. Len looked up and their gazes met across the short distance. At that moment, Joe knew it for what it really was: love.

He was in love with Len Crawford to a depth he'd never known. With that understanding, the drum heartbeat altered seamlessly into something else, something more. Right as Joe recognized the melody, Len crooned out the opening to Ruby & the Romantics' love ballad, *Our Day Will Come*.

Joe listened, unaware that he'd forgotten how to breathe until the last breath taken into his lungs boiled. Len sang on, and Joe knew the lyrics were for him, only him, because Len loved Joe as deeply.

"Our day will come," Joe whispered in tune with the song.

God help him, he welcomed it, wanted it, needed the young man's love. As Len reached the song's climax, Joe also understood that Len Crawford had both blessed and cursed him and that going forward, no one would ever arouse or consume him like the musician singing songs across a smoky room to the lone occupant of that corner table.

* * *

Their lips met, the kiss hard, verging on painful in its desperation. Joe cupped the back of Len's head in his palm and held on, not wanting to let go. He stiffened against the younger man and wondered if he'd ever softened since the Music Hall. Len moaned and melted into the protective shelter of Joe's arms. The cold night breeze streaming in past the opened car window had nothing on them.

"How was I?" Len asked untimed seconds or hours later when Joe surfaced from the kiss for air.

Smiling, he said, "Incredible!"

Len beamed, his joy visible in the wan glow offered by the streetlamps on North Amity. "The music, man."

"Yeah," Joe said while caressing Len's cheek with his right thumb.

Len leaned into his touch and trembled. Joe wasn't sure if the quiver owed to the night's chill or his touch's warmth—likely a mix of both, he decided.

"Joe," Len gasped, and again the speaking of his name sounded like a prayer. "Joe, I think ... I mean, I'm fairly certain that I ..."

"Me, too," Joe said.

Len's smile sagged before surging back to twice its intensity. "I love you."

There it was, given voice. The breeze gusted as the words swept around them before scattering into the night.

"Len," Joe sighed, the young man's name tasting sweet, "I love you. Oh, yes, I love you."

And then he proved it in actions as well as words with another kiss.

* * *

They snuck up the back stairs at Buxton Hall to the room at the corner. As Len explained, most of his fellow residents had gone home to their families for the weekend or were out getting into trouble. None, he guaranteed, were studying.

Joe crept up the stairs, his heart doing its best to jump out of his ribcage and into his throat. His inner voice reminded him that he'd gone on more dangerous forays on the far side of the universe.

They reached the room and Len closed the door. In that moment of darkness before Len switched on the desk lamp, Joe regretted his decision. But then the effulgence lit the small, private room, and standing at the center of the starburst was one of Heaven's angels. The most beautiful in all of creation.

Len said nothing, only smiled, and that more than seduced him. From the periphery, Joe drank in the details of single bed made hospital-crisp, the dresser, desk, and collection of musical instruments, everything neat and orderly. He recalled their rented cottage, still a mess of cardboard boxes and disarray.

Len sauntered over and wordlessly guided Joe's butt down to the bed. Saying nothing, he settled between Joe's legs and gazed up, surrendering all control. Or so Joe thought before Len reached for his big left foot and its sneaker. Joe tensed.

"No," Joe said.

Len remained where he was, poised to remove Joe's sneaker. "Why?"

Joe suffered a heat of embarrassment as it rose up the flesh of his throat. "Because."

"I bet you have handsome feet. You're a handsome man, Mister Devere," Len teased in a secretive tone. "That scent ... it's a real man's."

As he listened, bewitched, Len pulled off his sneaker and then the white sock beneath. The young man caressed the hairy skin above Joe's ankle while casting more powerful hocus-pocus.

"A secret about your feet," Len continued, his voice now close enough to Joe's toes that he felt the warmth of desperate sips of breath. "The nerves in your big, handsome feet are connected directly to those here ..."

Len reached between his legs. Joe moaned.

"That's why you curl your toes when you climax. So, you see, your feet are like two additional sex organs."

A DREAM WITHIN A DREAM

They certainly felt as though they were while Len worshipped them with kisses and licks.

They made something like love—twice. While on top of the young musician, connected by his hardness, Joe imagined they'd formed the perfect, all-male version of Yin/Yang. Nothing he'd known before had ever proved to be so fulfilling. He dared not think about anything after or about the numerous rules he'd broken until, soaked in a sweat that quickly cooled, he held Len in his protective embrace and pondered the bigger picture of the world beyond that little room.

Len hummed a siren's song—something elegiac that sounded like *Goin' Out of my Head* by Little Anthony and the Imperials. Sorrow replaced Joe's euphoria and sat icy in his stomach. "Don't go," he said.

Len glanced up and toyed with the hair on Joe's bare chest. "Go?"

"Away."

"Come with me," Len said. "Maybe the dream's big enough for the both of us."

"What?"

Len released the threads and touched Joe's chin. "Come with me to San Francisco. Suffer for art with me. We'll live in a world of music perfect for two in love."

"Yes," Joe said, unable to trap the promise or think about its cost. Because, over the course of the next second, he stole a glimpse of that other life spent with Len, and he knew it would be happy and fulfilling and worth all else he'd sacrifice in order to live it.

* * *

Fear rose cold through him. Joe pressed forward into the fog, aware of invisible ice cracking over his flesh, a haunted silence, and certainty that death was near because he was back there.

The jungle surfaced from the mist.

He was in uniform.

"No, no, God—not again!" he moaned, pleaded, the assault rifle like lead in his sweaty grip. At any second, the killing shot would tear into his chest or face. Blood would pour out, more to feed the swamp he navigated, this time alone. It was a familiar dream, one that always ended the same: with the telltale thunderclap and his eyes shooting open to a reality not much better. He'd wake soaked in clammy perspiration, race to the bathroom ahead of the surge of his vomit, sometimes make it while other times not.

But this dream continued.

Joe shot a look down in time to see his big, booted feet shift from swamp to solid ground. He'd come out of the quagmire. Ahead of him, water tumbled over time-smoothed rocks. The falls fed a grotto. An elephant frolicked in its crystalline pool. Purple orchids wreathed the giant's head.

Ganesha, Joe thought. *The Hindu god of new beginnings.* The elephant splashed, and though Joe knew such a thing impossible, it smiled before tossing back its enormous head and singing a pachyderm's version of hallelujah.

Joe glanced higher. A gray stone spire rose above the trees—an ancient temple scraping the humid sky.

No, the Music Hall!

Excitement thrummed through him. Its heat melted the ice. Joe hastened toward the temple. The jungle attempted to engulf him, so he ran faster, faster. He blinked and found himself at the Music Hall's doors, which stood open as though in invitation.

He stepped out of his boots and peeled off waterlogged socks, walking barefoot into the sacred space. En route to the stage, Joe looked down at that part of his anatomy he'd never considered attractive but now did because of Len. He saw that the rifle in his grip was a guitar—the old one in its case that he hadn't touched since before deployment.

He shed the last of his uniform and, naked, sat upon the stage and played—a few inelegant notes at first as he reacquainted his fingers and, more so, his soul with the music.

One of the wooden cherubs detached from the intricate carvings and floated down. "You're here," the angel said in Len's voice.

A DREAM WITHIN A DREAM

Joe ceased plucking. "Yeah. Thanks for pointing the way." He blinked, and the cherub was Len, naked and wreathed in purple orchids like the mysterious reveler at the waterfall. "Always before, this nightmare had a different ending," Joe said.

Len set his hand on Joe's bare leg. "To new beginnings, my love."

Joe resumed playing and wondered if all of his nights going forward would be exorcized of their demons.

Then he heard the thunderclap, and his eyes shot open. At first, he didn't recognize the room with its chaotic stacks of cardboard boxes.

* * *

She smoked her thin cigarettes in a huff and refused to meet his gaze. "I was alone the whole night," she accused. "Do you know how worried I was?"

"Work," he said, unable to offer more. The lie closed around him like a nightmare.

She stabbed out her cigarette in anger.

"Gia," he attempted.

She was beautiful, a wife that any man would be proud to claim as his own. But when she shot him that hateful look from across the table, she was more of a stranger to him than his own reflection.

"What aren't you telling me?" she demanded.

So much, he thought. *Heavenly Host forgive me, so very much.* "What's for dinner?" he asked instead.

* * *

Joe exhumed the relic from its sarcophagus. Len watched, his expression one of eager anticipation. Joe wondered what contributed more to that joy—the old, beat up guitar or its player. Both, he agreed. Len's Gibson was, as to be expected, perfectly tuned. Joe fumbled with his and ignored the vision his imagination attempted to paint of the two of them naked, guitars at the ready.

It was lunch break. A kind of extra credit. Nothing more. And yet, though unspoken, so much more.

"I'm ready," Joe said.

"You'll catch up, professor," Len said, his coyness so infuriating, so wonderful.

They played, nothing legit at first. But as the seconds and music continued, melodies aligned and actual music poured forth. The resplendent Indian Summer day beyond the classroom's open windows blessed them with a last kiss of autumn's warmth.

"Fall break," Len said between fret notes.

Joe glanced over. "Huh?"

"Escape."

It was real. He'd already taken stock of their finances. There wasn't much, but enough that she'd live comfortably until she figured out what she wanted to do, where she wished to go. Len's things and the little he planned to take would fit in the 'stang. No sweat. As for the rest ... he'd already suffered mightily, so what was doing the same for music in comparison to war?

"You and I," Joe said.

"I love you, Joe Devere," Len whispered.

And oh, the desire to kiss him right then, there, without caring who saw!

* * *

They made love.

Joe held Len close, the single bed in the dorm room uncomfortable but also glorious because it was Len's. From the gap of the opened window, the song of birds at twilight drifted in.

"That, the music ... I want us to create it," Len said.

Joe chuckled. "We can't. It's their music, not ours."

"We can try," Len said.

Joe leaned down and nipped at Len's mouth. He tasted the proof of his nectar on the younger man's lips.

A DREAM WITHIN A DREAM

"Sure, we can try."

* * *

Rain lashed the campus.

Joe parked in his usual spot and hurried into the main building. The chill worked through his suit coat, a first clue of the wrongness that would infect the day.

A commotion sounded outside the door between the end of third period and the start of the fourth. Raised voices and then shouts followed. "Guy—Devere," someone called.

By that point, Joe was through the door and operating on automatic. In quick order, he assessed the scrum taking place outside his classroom. Peck—Peck had someone against the wall. Like a pack of dogs, others of Hollings Head's finest had surrounded the aggressor and urged him on.

"You filthy homo!" Peck barked.

Joe shoved two students out of the way and seized hold of Peck's raised fist right as the young brute readied to launch his next savage punch. Joe hauled back and, in one fluid motion, had the aggressor behind him, the savaged before him. Len—Peck's previous knock had split his angel's lower lip.

Rage surged up Joe's throat. Howling, he drove Peck's backbone into the wall and fired a punch at the brute's face. Peck's nose shattered beneath his knuckles.

* * *

He sat in the dean's office being lectured to like one of his students.

"This is not how we behave at Hollings Head College, Mister Devere."

Joe flexed his fingers. The scrapes on his knuckles from hitting Peck's granite skull sang in agony, but how worth it that moment still was, how deeply satisfying. "The student in question was beating up another young man," Joe stated.

It wasn't much of a defense, and Dean Moody didn't cut him any breaks. "The student you assaulted had just learned that he'd been conscripted—the Lottery. Drafted, Mister Devere."

"That didn't give him the right to take out his anger on Len Crawford!"

"And it didn't give you the right to lay a hand on one of your students!"

For a terrible instant, Joe wasn't sure which student Dean Moody meant.

"I will review this fully, Devere," his interrogator said.

"You do that," Joe fired back, which earned him the dean's scowl. "And you remember that I served my two years over there while you're thinking about giving Peck a slap on the wrist."

"That'll be all, Mister Devere," Moody huffed.

Joe stood, flexed his right hand again and, saying nothing more, marched out of the dean's office and to his classroom, where he gathered his things.

It was over.

This life and its pretenses.

He didn't care.

They were leaving for something new.

* * *

The gray end-of-October breeze swept over Sugar Beach. Two lone figures braved the weather.

"My hero," Len said, his smile now marked by dried blood.

Joe exhaled and tucked his hands into his pockets. "If I was a hero, I'd have stopped Avimos Peck before he cornered you."

"Oh, he's not so tough," Len said lightly.

"Don't be kind to him."

Len shrugged. Far across Narragansett Bay, buoys tintinnabulated like bells, playing a sad melody.

"He's scared—and resentful that I didn't get called up. And won't because of, you know..."

Joe dug his bare feet into the cool, sugary sand and stopped. "You were meant for greater things."

Len faced him. "I was meant to meet a tall, strong soldier with an appreciation for music and fall madly, deeply, completely in love."

A DREAM WITHIN A DREAM

Joe's scowl broke. How could it not? "No one will ever hurt you again, babe."

They moved together, and Len fell into Joe's embrace. The future was far from certain, but love was. From somewhere unseen, a seabird sang its melancholy song, and October concluded.

* * *

Seated behind the wheel, he penned the letter. None of the words made the point cleanly, clearly. *It isn't you, Gia, it's me. You're better off without me. I'm dead. I died in that jungle.*

But there was a new Joe Devere. He'd been reincarnated since arriving to Hollings Head.

There's someone else.

He'd taken to sleeping on the sofa in the living room. She was already behind the fortress door of their former bedroom. He left the note and the checkbook on the kitchen table beside the glass ashtray, her packet of slim smokes, and the book of matches, where she was sure to find them. And with them, his wedding ring. It was gold. She could sell it.

Then, with a satchel full of clothes, his old guitar, and enough cash in his wallet for gas, food, and a few motel stops along the way between Here and There, he got back behind the wheel of the 'stang and drove to Buxton Hall to collect Len and begin their happy new life.

* * *

Joe drove, growing more anxious.

The coastal road that led into and out of town seemed to recede to a distance of light-years, not two quick left turns from campus. It glowed Stygian-black before his headlights. Finally, he reached his stop. Buxton Hall. The car idled. Joe waited for Len to appear. He rolled down the driver's side window and sucked in a cool, damp breath.

We're going to be so happy, Joe thought. *I'm so happy, truly happy, for the first time in my life.*

The heavens indulged him in the illusion for another few seconds before a thunderclap boomed and a shriek clawed through the still night air outside Buxton Hall. Joe jolted, convinced he was asleep and dreaming. The nightmare always ended in a gunshot. Only he was awake.

"Oh my God!" a male voice shouted. "What have you done? Peck, what have you done?"

Joe stumbled out of the car.

Avimos Peck burst through the door. In the light cast from the nearest streetlamp, Joe easily saw the blood, red and glistening, and how it had soaked the brute's face and coat. Peck still held the gun he'd used to commit the deed.

"Said he was leaving," Peck babbled after Joe tackled and disarmed him. "Leaving to make music and be in love. Why does *he* get that? Why?"

* * *

Joe gave his report to the police and, since his entire life was a façade, lied.

What were you doing here?

Apologizing for an incident that happened earlier in the week. You see, I went overseas, too.

With the blood still marking him, Joe entered the cottage.

She sat at the kitchen table smoking her slim cigarettes.

His letter was opened beside the glass ashtray.

Saying nothing, she got up, retreated to the bedroom, and quietly closed the door.

* * *

Rain hammered Hollings Head; a cold November rain that refused to break and turned everything bleak.

A DREAM WITHIN A DREAM

The shell of Joe Devere approached the coffin, which was closed. He remembered the terrible glimpse of the body he'd taken after his wrestle with Peck. The murderer's shot had disfigured Len's angelic face, making an open casket service impossible.

Joe stood among the mourning, aware of the rumpled state of his black suit and trousers, white button-down shirt, and black tie. He smelled his sweat and the stale dregs of beer upon his collar. The stares from the others suggested they were more upset by the fact he hadn't shaved than the casket's closed lid or the events that had led to this moment.

He swept the room through narrowed eyes, wondering which of the mourners among the staff and studentry were Len's uncle and family or if they'd bothered to attend at all.

"Wretches," Joe growled. "You loved him for his wealth but hated him for his pride!"

Hubert Weller stepped toward him. "Now, Devere, this isn't the time or proper place."

Joe held up his hand in warning. He'd already shown himself more than capable—twice—of taking down a college athlete, let alone some arrogant, tenured blowhard with a potbelly.

Weller halted his advance. Joe shook his head. Saying nothing, he plodded out of the funeral parlor and into the stormy night.

* * *

The rain fell.

Joe wandered along the path and ended up at the only place left.

The Music Hall towered above him, its spire seeming to stretch all the way past the storm and into the heavens.

"Len," Joe called. The rain smothered his voice. "Len!"

A night bird perched on the Music Hall's revetments cried back in elegy—a crow.

No, a raven, Joe realized.

He drew the length of black velvet ribbon and its key from his coat pocket and managed to insert it into the lock. The imposing doors groaned open, showing none of the elegant pitch to be found within the Music Hall's heart. He flipped on the lights. The chandeliers glowed. Dozens of carved wooden cherubs gazed down from the varnished walls, their bodies encased within wedding cake molding and rosettes.

"Len," Joe called out again. His voice rose up, up, to the distant ceiling. "Are you here, Len? Waiting for me, my angel?"

When no answer came, the tears spilled from Joe's eyes. His first in untold days and nights, they flowed and poured down his cheeks. The strength departed his legs and Joe dropped to the marble floor.

The howl powered up from his gut. Joe expelled it, and his cry lifted, transforming as it ascended, equal parts dirge and paean for Len, lost Len, the life gone from his eyes.

The death now upon his eyes.

And oh, how Joe's sob of mourning sounded like music, the most sorrow-filled of songs ever sung, as it carried aloft up to the King of Heaven.

USHER FALLS

The echo of every heartbeat fades,
and life's melody, like blood, becomes dust
—Author Unknown

Unknown, because it was spray-painted in red across the side of a tunnel wall. Stuck in traffic as I fought to get free of the city, those words taunted me. The car, three years old but still the newest ride I'd ever driven, idled and inched along. Left with no choice, I stole a glance at the backseat where clothes stuffed into garbage bags and everything I'd taken from the apartment were stacked—though 'stacked' was a generous term.

Tossed, I thought and again resisted the urge to lay on the horn.

Not that honking would have gotten me moving any faster. Someone farther back in the tunnel failed to grasp that basic truth and set off a chain reaction of blasts. I closed my eyes—for just a few seconds—and choked down a dry swallow while waiting for the ominous effect at my back to run its course. When I opened them again, my haunted gaze stared back from the rearview along with the toaster. The toaster—I'd taken it because I bought it and it was still on the kitchen counter after my two roommates had cleared out. In the wild panic of packing up to escape Boston, I'd grabbed the toaster but not the loaf of rye bread or any of the things on the top shelf in the closet. Very clearly, I saw the apple-green photograph box with old family snapshots and other of my life's relics overlooked and abandoned. Considering what was happening, I doubted I'd ever return to the city. But at least I'd remembered to take the toaster.

My cell, plugged into the charging cord, buzzed. I woke from my spell of thoughts and automatically stabbed the answer button. The screen lit and an unfamiliar face appeared.

"Hello. This is Doctor Alvin Kendricks, Chief Virologist of the Commonwealth of Massachusetts," the man addressed me in a calm, metered voice. "As you know, Crimson has been detected in our state. We in the Governor's Office are doing all we can and request the same of you. If you don't need to travel, we strongly urge you to shelter at home. Wear a mask when you're forced to head out for groceries or important medical appointments. We ask that you limit interactions with others as we attempt to get through this. And we will—together."

I stabbed the end call button. More honking sounded, this time close enough that I jumped. It was right on my rear bumper. I looked up and saw that the line ahead of me was moving. I gave my car some gas and raced forward.

A start, they were calling it. But given the empty grocery shelves, long lines at gas stations that had jacked up prices, and the abandoned vehicles I spotted after picking up Route 2 and leaving Boston, it looked more like an ending.

* * *

Come to Usher Falls, the text had read. **Ride out the winter here. It's a big house w/everything we need. And I could use the company, my dear friend.**

By then, the news was getting grimmer. Rosie, my coworker, had already fled the apartment and gone north to Maine. My other roommate, Ginny, south to family on the Cape. I'd paced the apartment, cursing the many times I'd dreamed about what it would be like to have the place all to myself. I couldn't afford the rent on my own—not that rent was the biggest issue now, not with Crimson having landed on the shores of the Bay State.

I paced. Messages streamed in over my cell from the mayor and governor's offices, urging citizens to stock up on necessities and expect service interruptions in the coming weeks. With rent likely going unpaid and heating oil thrice the cost of the previous winter, I wondered how long it was until the landlord cut off the

A DREAM WITHIN A DREAM

furnace. September had started unseasonably chilly and had ended on an even brisker note.

Then the text from Regina.

Please agree, Helaine, I am unwell, as you might guess. But having you here will do wonders for my spirit!

I'd known Regina since we were children, both attending the company's daycare. She was the rich daughter of the C.E.O. of Usher Pharmaceuticals, me the poor kid of a single mom who'd worked her way up to lower management. Reggie never treated me like an underling and, once, I'd traveled with her to Paris on her insistence the summer after her big brother died. We'd dined at sidewalk cafes and toured the Louvre together in a time that now seemed part of some other life.

Usher Falls: the town named long ago for its most prominent and influential family. Winter at the Usher Estate. Ride out this Crimson pandemic.

Traffic thinned. I tipped a nervous look down at the gas tank to see I had just over a half left following my slow escape from the city and hoped it would be enough. I traveled west—toward the deep Berkshires—as the day grayed and exhaustion threatened to overwhelm me. While still located in the urban sprawl, I passed a car with out of state plates pulled over to the side of the road by a police cruiser whose lights flashed in silence. *At least I won't hit checkpoints*, I told myself, and continued forward, one fragile step ahead of my tears.

* * *

I hadn't seen Reggie Usher in years apart from on social media, which she infrequently updated. The last new photograph she posted was an artsy silhouette—which was very much her style—in blue light that washed out most of her frail features. A lock of blonde hair hung over the side of her thin face. That selfie was over four years old, long before the Crimson.

I dialed up my playlist instead of listening to the radio, which was all bad news all the time, and attempted to focus on the near future. *There's a handyman. Takes care of the house and me I suppose. Other than that, we'll have the place to ourselves. I* recalled her message. *We'll pretend we're in the Louvre, only this time no snooty chaperones or security guards shooting us looks!*

"It'll be fun," I whispered aloud.

But even then, still so far from reaching my destination, I didn't believe it.

I glanced at the dashboard clock. For a terrifying instant, the numbers weren't there, seeming to indicate time had run out. I blinked and saw that it was just after one. The clogged arteries leading out of the city made it conceivable I wouldn't reach Usher Falls before dusk, which arrived earlier each night as the days grew shorter. My next breath hitched in my throat. I cracked the window. Icy air rushed in, shocking me back to clarity.

I drove on.

* * *

The sun dipped near the tops of the thickening trees, many of which showed a blood spatter pattern of turning foliage. I was lost, surely I'd traveled past the Massachusetts border, sped through New York State, Canada, and the known world. This single-lane road, one of numerous turns off Route 2, likely led to a dead end.

With my heart bouncing inside my ribcage like a trapped animal, I continued forward. The trees thinned enough that I spied the river. Something Reggie had said about the first sign I was getting close broke through my panic. A few houses appeared, old ranches and New Englanders, and then what passed for a small downtown—a hardware store, diner, post office, a few mom & pops, and, farther along, the Lower Falls.

I pulled over, drank in a cleansing breath, and then neared the final leg of my long journey. Few were out and about even here, far from the crowded eastern edge of Massachusetts. The diner and hardware store both posted CLOSED signs in their front windows. I picked up the paved road running past the Lower Falls and traveled it until it turned to dirt. Not far beyond, I stole my first look at the imposing house of the Usher family, and that brief feeling of relief at not being lost as night came on extinguished like the flame of a candle quietly blown out.

A DREAM WITHIN A DREAM

It rose above the banks of the Upper Falls, what I at first thought to be an indestructible fortress made of ancient timbers and stone blocks. The spray drifting up in a miasma from the falling water cloaked the estate in an added layer of grayness, making it seem only half there, a ghost.

I neared, crossing the stone bridge over a chasm, and up to the wrought iron gate that separated the sprawling grounds from the rest of the town—the rest of the world. Staring through the ancient, decorative bars in their pattern of grape vines, leaves, and fruit, another impression formed; that the house had long decayed within its perch beside the Upper Falls, and only mortar kept the dust of those stone blocks from collapsing; only paint held the rotted timbers intact.

I studied it, my revulsion growing. Mullioned windows leered back like dozens of eyes. The numerous turret rooms and untold dark corners contained within the estate unleashed a shiver down my backbone. I imagined stagnant spaces, putrefaction ... and I drove hours to be safe at this place. Once I stepped through the front entrance, I'd be trapped.

Run, my inner voice pleaded. *Now—before it's too late to change your mind!* I almost heeded it. Almost turned around in the narrow approach beyond the stone bridge leading up to the sealed gate. But a glance down at the gas gage showed I was under a quarter of a tank. I hadn't passed a gas station since ... Route 2? The sun was setting, and I had nowhere else to go.

Nowhere but the big, brooding house in Usher Falls.

I reached for my phone, intending to text: **I'm here.** But I had no service. The message cycled, urging me to send at a later time. I thought about leaning on the horn. Then, in the day's waning light, I spied the intercom set beside the gate. I got out of my car and stepped into the October chill. The roar of the falls thrummed around me, through me. I felt the echo in my molars, my marrow, and wondered how long it would take before the constant pulse drifted into the background like traffic noises on a busy street. Or would I go mad from that heavy, constant din before I adjusted to it?

I thumbed the intercom. "Hello, it's me—Helaine. I'm here."

I waited.

Nothing.

"Reggie? I'm outside at the main gate. I'm pretty sure I've got the right place."

I straightened and laughed, though the sound lacked all humor and struck my own ear like the chuckle of a lunatic. High over the house of the Usher family, the moon rose, seeming to study me like a narrowed eye.

No response came through the intercom, but I heard the gate release and its two halves opened, beckoning me to enter. I got back into my car and drove through. Behind me, the gates resealed, and I tried to not think I'd been swallowed whole by the estate. More so, that I would never again leave through that rusting gate.

I had arrived, and I was a prisoner.

* * *

The long, winding drive leading up to the main house passed through a cathedral of ancient oaks. I spotted several outbuildings—what I assumed had once been stables for horses and a greenhouse whose glass roof had collapsed some long while before my visit. Except for the lawn closest to the great house, the acreage was overgrown and going wild.

The circular drive led up to the house, beneath a portico and the gaze of those many windows. My worry deepened. Two cars were parked there, one a new-model luxury vehicle, the other more beat-up, an SUV with torque, a man's kind of ride.

The handyman's, I thought.

No sooner had I made the connection than I saw him, hastening down from the front door to greet me. He matched his wheels—rugged, blue collar in old jeans, a frayed flannel shirt that showed the sculpt of the torso beneath, flattop, old work boots and five o'clock shadow showing on a weathered, handsome face right on schedule.

I had to admit it—older, and yet I found him instantly desirable. My revulsion for my surroundings ebbed as I got out of the car.

"Helaine Wandry?" he asked, his gruff voice in synch with the rest of the image presented.

A DREAM WITHIN A DREAM

"The one and only." Then I realized my big social slip and reached for my paper mask. "You're—?"

"Derry. Roderick Derry," he said. "And you don't have to. It's only us here."

I pulled on the mask only to again remove it and grabbed my tote while he attempted to make sense of the jumble of bags, cases, and whatnot tossed helter-skelter in the backseat and trunk.

"Quite a place," I said, spurred on by nerves and the sudden absence of sound other than the distant chug of the Upper Falls.

He looked up, flashed a crooked, spare smile, and offered me a tip of his chin in response, that universal greeting unique to men. Saying nothing more, holding onto my luggage in one hand, a trash bag filled with clothes in the other, and that ridiculous toaster under his arm, he led the way up to the house's imposing double doors.

Those doors opened onto a marble foyer. Past the inner vestibule doors, the grand scope of the manor spread. Far above me were patterned plaster ceilings and long beams of ancient timber. Chandeliers draped in crystals hung down, though none were lit, and even the many windows did little to temper the gloom that filled the cavernous vastness.

As I walked inside I saw portraits and large photographs lining a gallery wall—the Usher family, I guessed. A varnished staircase soared up to the second floor landing, which led away in two directions. That smell of age I'd imagined back in my car was there, but as I followed the handyman deeper into the house and up those stairs, I caught a note of his scent—the dregs of deodorant, maybe body spray, mixed with clean, masculine sweat—and my attraction toward him doubled. Maybe it was just desperation disguised as desire.

"You live here?" I asked, my voice broadcast twice as loudly as I'd meant it to in the vastness around us.

"I have a room downstairs," Roderick said.

Roderick Derry—a manly sort of name for a manly sort of man. I liked it.

"You've got the Blue Room," he added on our tromp left down the second-floor hallway.

"Let me guess—because...?"

"It's blue," he said.

I caught more of that crooked smirk and, unable to stop the thought from crossing my exhausted mind, wondered what it would be like to kiss his mouth. And more.

We passed through an odd space—an oblong expanse with a few chairs and a guitar set neatly upon a stand. Tall windows inset high in the wall barely permitted the last of the day's light. The room seemed located at the center of the main house.

"Reggie?" I asked, my voice echoing through the oblong box even on low volume.

"Napping. I'll let her know you're here when she wakes up," Roderick said.

"Napping?"

"She gets tired easily."

"Oh."

We approached another stretch of hallway, this carpeted in threadbare rugs that must have been exquisite when new. For a terrible moment, I saw myself getting lost in the maze of rooms. A few doors down, Roderick stopped. We'd reached the Blue Room—and, as its name promised, the place was blue.

Robin's egg paint on the walls, a large four-post bed with canopy dominated one half of the room. Two Queen Anne chairs upholstered in cobalt velvet were arranged in front of a stone fireplace. Heavy curtains on the windows nearly blocked the dying sunset. The ceiling seemed to be a thousand miles above my head. A chill pervaded the room. I couldn't tell if it was the actual temperature or me.

Roderick set down my bags. "I'll build a fire," he said after tracking my gaze.

I flashed a brave smile.

"Then I'll grab the rest of your things."

I watched him work as he methodically stacked stove-lengths over newspaper and tried my best not to think of him as the one who'd chopped and split that firewood, sweating with his shirt off, the scent of the wood hot atop his glistening flesh. I wanted to beat myself up for undressing a complete stranger but couldn't. The wheels had come off the world. We were at an ending point, I knew. What was left but crumbs of happiness, even the illusion of joy, where I could find it?

A DREAM WITHIN A DREAM

He cleared his throat. The fire took. I smelled its fresh, sharp scent curling around him and fell deeper into something like a crush for the estate's handyman.

Roderick flashed another small smile, and oh, how attractive it looked on his weathered face. "There."

"There," I parroted.

He nodded, said nothing more, and left me alone in the Blue Room.

* * *

I emerged from the attached bathroom to see all of the sad relics of my life stacked at the foot of the enormous bed. After my long trip, I appreciated Reggie's need for naps. I locked the bedroom door, slipped off my sneakers, and crawled onto the top of the bedspread feeling dwarfed by my new accommodations. The comforter smelled of lavender and something that could only have been the staleness of age.

Tears came suddenly and without warning. Part of it was exhaustion, I'm sure. The rest?

A chill prickled over my flesh. I was far from all that was familiar during what was now labeled the end of time.

Usher Pharm is working on a cure for the Crimson, Reggie had texted when I was still pacing the apartment in Boston. **We'll be among the first to be protected when the vaccine gets Federal approval** ...

So why didn't I feel safe or hopeful? I drifted to sleep but soon jolted awake. The fire crackled behind its elegant brass screen. In a fetal curl, I barely felt any warmth.

A knock sounded on the outside of my bedroom door. I sat up and wiped my eyes on my sleeve. "Reggie?"

"No, Roderick," he spoke through the locked door.

I eased my feet back into my sneakers and answered. Roderick stood on the other side of the threshold looking even more magnificent than his last visit to my room.

"Reggie's awake. She'd like to see you. And dinner's almost ready, but ..." His voice trailed to a sigh, the sentence left unfinished.

"But?"

"You should know, she's on a very bland diet. Gluten free. No seasoning."

I listened but didn't really hear the meaning between his words. "It's okay. I'm not really hungry."

"I can bring up a salt shaker. I'd dump the stuff on mine if not for—"

Again, he left the thought dangling. I waved it off. He leaned against the doorframe, arms folded, and for the first time, seemed to notice me. Warmth ignited in my belly and drove out the lingering chill. I liked his attention.

"Come on," Roderick said. He led the way down the hallway, and I followed.

This room was painted in yellows. At one time, the colors might have appeared cheery, but by that dusk, they'd not faded as much as soured, becoming strangely acidic like the stain of rodents. Windows similar to mine ran along the tops of the walls. A fire crackled within the bricks of the room's hearth. A dusty smell hung over the space.

What had to be a dozen bottles of pills and potions covered a nightstand just beyond the bed's canopy of Bavarian lace. The room's occupant and mistress of the house, Regina Clare Usher, sat upright on the bed, her cell phone and an ancient book set beside her, contrasts in time. The Then and the Now. From what I could see of her beyond the Bavarian lace veils draped over the bed, she was as slender as always. A black velvet ribbon held her hair in a tail. But that hair ...

She was a natural blonde, and when we were younger, I admit, I coveted her hair color. Now, I had the sense that Reggie's hair had thinned. Her skin looked pallid, the body in that big bed frail, only half there.

"Helaine?" she mewled.

"Reggie," I said, attempting to disguise my shock at her condition. "Oh, Reg."

I stepped closer. Reggie held up a hand in warning. I moved no closer.

"I forgot my mask," I said.

Reggie laughed. "Masks ... I'm afraid this has nothing to do with the Crimson but everything to do with genetics. That royal, blue Usher blood of mine."

I shrugged.

"Sit, Helaine. I'm so thrilled you've joined us here at the family estate."

A DREAM WITHIN A DREAM

Roderick carried over one of the tufted chairs from in front of the fire and I sat, sinking into its aged comfort.

"I'll let you catch up while I fetch dinner," he said and left us.

I faced Reggie. "What is it?"

"Something you'd think there'd be a cure for, given, well, the Ushers—we made our fortune on medicines and snake oils. But it's a condition caused by the Ushers. How's that for dramatic irony, Helaine?"

I didn't know what to say, so I stayed silent.

"There are some lovely side effects," she continued. "Has the handyman told you about dinner?"

I waved a hand.

"No Parisian gourmet treats, I fear. My stomach can't handle anything with actual taste. And do you see a single flower anywhere in this house?"

I hadn't.

"The smell makes me instantly nauseous. So, too, does music of any kind except the guitar. Everything else strikes my ear like thunder. It sounds horrible, I know—and likely makes you want to turn around and leave."

I offered a smile. "Of course not."

"Good. Because once you're here, you can't leave. We're isolating until the Crimson passes or our people crack the cure. They're working around the clock. Until then, we have everything we need here and plenty of it. And we'll have fun!"

She said this, and I almost believed her, until she broke into a coughing fit, and it struck me that I was seated beside a living ghost.

* * *

He wheeled in the dining cart, a metal contraption with two plates under cloches. Roderick served Reggie first. In silence, I studied his gentle movements as he sat her up, unfolded a wooden tray with legs over her lap, and served her one of the offerings. With Reggie attended to, he carried over a table from the suite near the fireplace and set my dinner upon it along with a crystal water goblet, linen napkin, silverware, and the promised salt shaker. He winked, and I surrendered more of my confused heart to the Usher's handyman, a stranger.

"Thank you, Roderick," I said.

Reggie chuckled, the sound throaty, awful to hear. "I'd reserve your thanks until you check out the limited menu."

I removed the cloche. The plate contained various mashes and purees. I identified the potatoes and applesauce by sight. The green glop could have been anything. Both Reggie and her manservant had been correct in warning me the food had zero taste. I doused it all with salt, surprised at how hungry I'd become even for this.

Reggie dined slowly. She uncapped medicine bottles, downing pills along with antacids, and from the cut of my eye, I noted the paleness of her hand, those fingers adorned in rings, one boasting the biggest ruby I'd ever seen.

* * *

"We'll play the guitar in the conservatory," she said.

"That space outside my room?"

Reggie nodded. "And there's a media room—though hardly full of what you'd think of as streaming content. And there are books and a gym downstairs."

I listened, my exhaustion back. "It all sounds great. I'm just happy to be out of the madness."

"Madness?"

I looked up. Reggie's pale blue eyes were fixed on me without blinking from behind the lace canopy.

"Of the city. The outside world. Tell me—is it as bad as I think?"

"The Crimson? Oh, it's worse. Much, much worse."

Silence settled over the room, a pall broken only by the background crackle of the fireplace and something I hadn't noticed until that moment: the falls, spilling unseen beyond the house's walls.

"I'm tired," Reggie said. "Perhaps tomorrow ..."

A DREAM WITHIN A DREAM

I stood, also tired from my tense drive to get here. "Good night, Reggie—and thanks again."

She nodded. I started to gather the plates with their congealing stains, but she stopped me.

"No, leave that for Roderick."

"Are you sure?"

"Quite. Goodnight, Helaine."

I wandered out of the Yellow Room and into the hallway. I passed the metal cart parked in front of the open door of a dumbwaiter I hadn't noticed on my maiden voyage to see Reggie. I hoped to encounter Roderick but didn't. I made my way back through the conservatory to my room.

Outside the door, I listened. Stillness lay over the vast house. I entered my room. The fire had burned down to embers. En route to adding more wood, I doubled back and locked the door.

Sleep claimed me almost immediately, yet throughout the night I jolted awake unable to shake the fear I imagined creeping in like something physical from the shadows.

* * *

I woke to a gray morning at the end of the world and showered. The soap provided was a bland-smelling brand with no added fragrance. I looked at the freesia shampoo I'd brought along, my favorite, and decided to use the soap instead to wash my hair out of respect for Reggie and what she'd told me about the fragrance of flowers. My hope was that rested eyes and a new day might alter my perception of the great house of the Family Usher, but when I stepped out into the hall, the gloom was still everywhere, even thicker now because I was there and stuck.

I put on a bright face and skipped down the soaring staircase. No breakfast smells lured me toward what I assumed was quite the well-outfitted kitchen. I mean—the house had a dumbwaiter!

I navigated another long hallway and passed many doors, wondering which led to the handyman's room. One stood open, and I heard his grunts coming from inside. I glanced in to see the aforementioned gym and Roderick Derry working out. My next breath came with difficulty. In quick order, I absorbed the room's details—weight benches, weights, a workout mat, and a few strength and conditioning machines set before a wall's length of mirror that also sported a bar, the kind for ballet stretches.

Even quicker, I recorded the details of Roderick.

Apart from the pair of black sweatbands on his wrists, the only stitch of clothes he had on was a pair of khaki cargo shorts with those big pockets. In the middle of lifting hand weights, he growled and sweated. Perspiration soaked his chest, which was as magnificent as I'd guessed beneath the cover of his flannel shirt. His legs glistened. The right calf bore a smiling sundial tattoo in blue. Even the man's big feet were attractive in a way that part of the male anatomy wasn't normally considered.

Transfixed, I stared. At one point, he noticed me, looked up, and smiled.

"Morning," I blathered.

Roderick nodded, set down the weights and straightened, his big hands riding low on the inch or so of bare hip above his unbelted cargo shorts.

"Uh," I said. "Is there coffee?"

Roderick's grin widened. "And if there isn't?"

"If there isn't? All bets are off. I'll take my chances out there with the Crim—" I'd meant it to be light but caught myself.

"Regina can't drink coffee, only the most boring kinds of tea," he said, crushing me. "Even the smell of it makes her sick."

In the next moment, I drank down a breath and indulged in his scent of sweat, which smelled like summer rain.

"However," he said, his smirk ending as he reached for a towel to mop his face. "Some of us still need our Morning Joe. Hope you don't mind instant, and we need to drink it only in the kitchen."

He wiped his face and chest. On his way toward the door, he surprised me yet again by performing the most athletic of moves—hands down, legs up. In the breathless moment that followed, Roderick made a handstand and walked three steps closer, his moves graceful and perfectly balanced.

A DREAM WITHIN A DREAM

And more attractive than I thought possible.

A few steps shy of the door, he jumped back down. "Coffee, Helaine?"

* * *

He drew on another old button-down but didn't button it. The coffee barely exuded a smell in a kitchen that had to have been an acre in size. The doors were closed to hold in any possible scent escaping. Most of the appliances were older, white. A note of mustiness I guessed was permanent infused the place. But the instant brew, up close, dispelled it.

"How did you sleep?" he asked.

"You know," I shrugged, "strange bed in a strange house."

He chuckled. "This is a strange one."

I took to one of the stools set before the length of white marble counter at the center island. It wasn't particularly comfortable. Roderick offered sugar and shelf-stable milk in a box. I took mine black.

"We won't run out of instant coffee or anything else," he said. "There's an entire warehouse of food in cans and boxes. I made sure to stock up on coffee."

"Amen," I said and sipped.

For instant, the coffee was robust and delicious. Unlike our hostess at Usher House, I felt myself come alive from this single indulgence. We drank our coffee. He held his cup like a modern day caveman with his long fingers wrapped around the bowl. It was sort of nice. Comforting, anyway. Something I could grow used to. Morning coffee with the estate's handsome handyman here at the end of the world.

"How long have you worked here?" I asked.

Roderick shrugged. "Who knows?"

Further proof that time no longer mattered. My new life at Usher House operated under different parameters.

I caught his scrutiny and loved it.

"So, is there anyone?" he asked.

"Anyone?"

He tipped his chin at the line of windows, indicating the greater world beyond. "You know, out there."

"My mom died three years ago."

"I'm sorry."

"Thanks."

"Boyfriend?"

"Not since ..." I didn't finish the statement. It was more *who knows?* in a land without time. "So what's on the schedule for today?"

"Breakfast first," he said. "Then ..."

I waited for him to finish his answer. He didn't and instead fixed us another instant coffee. Yes, I could get used to my mornings with Roderick Derry.

* * *

Breakfast was eggs, toast with jam, and wedges of fresh orange. I ate at the island while Roderick fixed egg whites in a scramble, toast without butter, and no fruit, no coffee, only bland tea for Regina. He carried the plate away, leaving me alone in the vast kitchen. I stole a look at the network of big solar panels lined up along a part of the grounds near the main house. The background chug of the falls returned in the absence of our conversation.

I walked my coffee over to the nearest of the windows. Past the modern solar panels lurked a feature from an earlier epoch. I narrowed my gaze to see a fence of wrought iron beyond where the lawn had been mowed. Trees had grown around the fence.

A cemetery, I realized. The graves of the Ushers. A chill teased the nape of my neck. I fought it, failed. The shiver spilled down my spine.

* * *

Left to my own means, I explored the downstairs of my new living space. An iciness embraced most of the house past the thresholds of closed doors, the crystal knobs cold to the touch.

A DREAM WITHIN A DREAM

I located the media room which boasted not only a theater-sized flat-screen TV but also all manner of relics—a VHS player, a movie projector with reels, and shelves filled with film canisters.

In another corner of the downstairs, I came across the library. Bookshelves capped by intricate carvings of acanthus leaves stretched far over my head, the upper stacks accessible by rolling ladders. An enormous globe of the Earth stood frozen in its orbit before French doors leading out to a courtyard. There were chairs upholstered in merlot-colored velvet, a work table, and a roll-top desk. At least a million books filled the space.

I continued my exploration. The adventure made me feel like a young girl again, curiosity leading the way and all gloom forgotten for a while. I circled back toward the kitchen to check out the dining room. At the formal dining room's center was an oblong table that could seat sixteen, though the room, with its faded peacock print wallpaper, hadn't known those kinds of numbers since long before my time at Usher House. Reggie was the last of the line.

I wandered over to the gallery and its many portraits and photographs. The severe, harsh faces captured in oils from long ago days all bore what I'd come to think of as the Usher Look—thin profiles, blue gazes, and blonde hair. Photographs in black and white carried the resemblance into color. I located Reggie, first as a young girl and then her high school graduation photo at the very end of the line. One step before the denouement of the Family Usher was a framed 8 x 10 of a young boy. He wore a harsh expression and a blue bowtie.

The brother, I thought. *The one Reggie said used to bay at the moon. The one who tried to kill himself and eventually succeeded.* I stared into the boy's blue eyes. They were as cold and dead as the rest of the gallery of ghosts.

"Helaine?" Roderick called, shocking me out of my thoughts.

I looked up. Roderick stood at the top of the staircase, still magnificent in those cargo shorts and his barely-buttoned shirt.

"Reggie—she'd like it if you joined her in the conservatory."

* * *

It wasn't much of an actual music room. The conservatory lacked a piano despite having plenty of space for one, and no artwork decorated the bare walls. I wondered if that latter fact owed to resonance—if everything but the guitar jagged on Reggie's ear, the openness made a kind of insane sense.

Reggie sat in one of the chairs, the guitar in her feeble grasp. She was dressed in a pale green satin robe that added to the pallor of her flesh. Without the veil of her bed canopy, Reggie's thinning hair and emaciated body materialized clearly. She flashed a harsh expression that matched the ones in the gallery.

"You thought I was acting," she laughed. "That I was making up all of this sickness."

I remembered the many times we'd dabbled in the arts—poetry, painting, playwriting, and acting, none of it very serious, nothing permitted to be before we moved on to our next dalliance. "No," I lied.

"I remember your voice—so beautiful," Reggie said. She reached into her pocket and removed a folded slip of paper. "You sing while I play."

I unfolded the sheet. Written in elegant cursive were the lines of a song she'd written and obsessed over. Reggie strummed on the guitar, and the walls sent the music back in soft, dreamy echoes. I jumped in and sang.

The Empty Palace

I.

Empty are its many rooms,
This vast and tragic palace.
Not so empty, certain tombs
Those filled with tears and malice.

A DREAM WITHIN A DREAM

II.

The palace wasn't always so—
An endless realm of sorrow.
The girl recalls new morning's glow
Before she reached tomorrow.

III.

Running, laughing, through its halls,
Oblivious in her joy.
The eyes that stared down from the walls—
Her soul they wished to destroy.

IV.

The palace built beside the water
Held her screams within.
She, the last-born Usher daughter
No one there to hear the din.

V.

She, the sole remaining Usher
The Fates so cruel and callous!
The family curse, soon doomed to crush her
Within that empty palace.

"Again!" Reggie said, more demand than request.

We performed the piece half a dozen more times that morning until her exhaustion caught up and she crept away to the Yellow Room.

* * *

I hopped onto the exercise bike and built up a decent sweat. After an hour, my hope that Roderick would join me in a morning workout faded.

Disappointed, I wandered up the stairs to my bedroom to shower and dress for breakfast. At the door, I heard what could have been sobs or laughter echoing from the direction of the conservatory. But when I poked my head in for a look, no one was there.

* * *

A cold rain hammered the house. The storm's chill worked through the walls and timbers, and not even the fire roaring in my bedroom dispelled it.

I slipped into a sweater. A knock sounded at the door.

Roderick stood outside, his handsomeness warming me more than the cashmere. "Cold?" he asked.

"A little."

"I'll turn up the heat. But Reggie, you know, she gets sensitive when it's too much one way or the other."

"I'm fine."

He hovered at the threshold. "She wants to see you."

I nodded and made my way down the long hallway to her chamber. I knocked. Reggie called for me to enter. When I did, I found her counting out candy-colored pills from her pharmacopeia and washing them down with a glass of water.

"You need something?" I asked.

"Yes. Certain books from the library," she said and produced a sheet of paper, the titles written out by hand.

I scanned the list. *The Noctum Celebratum*, *Lizor's Magicks*, *The Cathedral of Thorns*, *The View Beyond the Aperture*, and others with peculiar names were spelled out in Reggie's elegant cursive.

The chill was back, this time worse. "The library? It's huge. I wouldn't know where to look."

A DREAM WITHIN A DREAM

"You won't have any difficulty finding the titles in this particular collection." She handed me an old skeleton key. "They're locked separately from the others. *Entombed.*"

I hesitated about taking the key. Outside, the wind howled around Usher House, scattering rain across those tall upper windows.

"My older brother, when he took his own life," Reggie continued in a voice barely louder than a whisper. "It was winter, the ground frozen. They stored his body in the cellar. My mother, unable to bear the tragedy, insisted he be interred there forever so as to be closer to us than he would in the family plot. He's still down there, Helaine, behind the walls. Some nights, I swear I hear him howling at the moon, laughing, crying ..."

The insanity in her words struck me and fully registered for the first time.

Madness, I thought while accepting the key.

There'd been the brother, I remembered on my slow march down the staircase, and surely, the entire line of Ushers, suffering from one level or form of mental illness or another. When I considered Reggie's declining health at so young an age, I wondered if there was more behind her determination. The Usher Curse mentioned in her song—hereditary? All those blonde locks and blue eyes memorialized on the gallery wall ...

I entered the library and found it even colder than the rest of the house. Outside, the rain hammered on the panes. I switched on the lights only to rethink that decision. A strange paranoia gripped me—the slither of unwanted eyes from somewhere beyond the house, in the storm. The cast iron radiators ticked. True to Roderick's promise, he'd cranked the heat.

Remembering the key, I searched the stacks for a locked door, at first finding none. Then, far overhead, I noticed a barrister's shelf in one dark corner. Dizziness possessed me before I rolled the library ladder over and set foot on the bottom step.

The dead brother's corpse, entombed in the cellar. Still down there. He used to bay at the moon.

I closed my eyes, focused, and gripped the key along with Reggie's list. Six books, all from a locked cabinet separated from the rest of the vast library, those books devoted to the macabre and otherworldly. I ascended. Was I enabling her madness? How could I refuse?

For an instant, that locked vault existed as high up as the tallest of Usher House's three circle towers. The wind outside the room moaned in a disembodied voice and scattered the rain in long sheets. What felt like minutes later—hours—instead of seconds, I reached the top of the rolling ladder. In years long past, I could imagine Reggie and I would have been racing back and forth like horse riders on that rolling, wrought iron contraption and likely getting punished for doing so. Now, my presence in the room was wholly somber. I reached a shaking hand and inserted the skeleton key. The lock resisted. I tried again. This time, the lock turned and released.

I lifted the door up and rolled it into its recess. A smell of age wafted out, unpleasant to my nose, not the usual vanilla of old books but something mildewed, rotten. I peered into the dark alcove. Many an ancient volume was housed in the reliquary of that locked shelf. I located the six books my hostess had requested, locked the cabinet, and started down.

Several steps before reaching the bottom, my right foot slipped. In that splintered instant, I saw myself sprawled and bleeding, bones broken, and no medical help likely apart from that found inside this prison setting where the inmates were given an illusion of freedom to move about.

Roderick caught me.

I landed in his strong, protective arms and looked up and into his crooked smile, still visible in the expanding shadows.

"Whoa," he said.

I again detected his scent of clean skin, sweat, and rain mixed with the dregs of either deodorant or body spray on my next desperate breath.

"You okay?" he asked.

I started to answer—*I am now*. Instead, I kissed him.

Our lips connected at an awkward angle. The kiss verged on painful in its desperation. We separated, and the most crushing sense of defeat filled me until Roderick cupped my cheek and our lips met again, this time in a fit that proved to be glorious.

A DREAM WITHIN A DREAM

Somehow, still holding those foul books, I reached my free hand behind him, circled his back, and held on. Our mouths again parted, the kiss cursed to be brief inside this empty palace. The hand on my cheek remained there for several more seconds, long enough for Roderick to brush his thumb across my lips. He smiled again, the gesture spare, but it was enough.

"You sure you're all right?" he asked, his voice husky with desire.

I nodded. "Sure am."

He flashed a look, those blue eyes not entirely confident but filled with boyish mischief. They seemed to predict the promise of fun yet to be experienced and some small joy for the future I'd already written off as gone. Saying nothing more, he slipped away from me and out of the room. The scuffle of his soles across the floor wove a kind of melody that fueled my arousal.

"Roderick," I sighed, but he was gone.

The unpleasant weight in my arms reminded me of my mission. I wanted to pursue my rescuer. Instead, I plodded back up the staircase and down the long hallway to Regina's sickroom.

* * *

On a day not long after that—though it could have been weeks, given that time lost most of its meaning in the house of the Ushers—I pulled on my heavy coat and tromped outside into the end-of-autumn chill. Frost had thickened on the dead stalks of grass. Ice crunched beneath my boots. The next precipitation would fall as snow, according to the plummeting temperature. To my right, the river that fed the falls chugged past. I reached the solar panels feeling gratitude that no matter what happened in the outside world, we would have energy for food and light.

Far beyond in the day's gray glow, my destination loomed: the cemetery of the Family Usher.

I'd hoped my excursion outside would help me to breathe easier than being walled up inside the old house. The notion of long winter months bottled within the manor was making sleep difficult. I often startled awake fighting for air that refused to come easily. Black mold? The house had sat on the banks beside the falls for centuries; the air was always damp. I recalled theories that it had been mold responsible for the witchcraft hysteria in Salem far to the east of my present location. Was black mold behind the Usher Curse? At least part of it? If so, had it infected me?

I reached the rusting, wrought iron gate leading into the private cemetery. A few dozen markers rose up from the frozen ground, some made of white marble and so old that the names and relevant dates had melted away thanks to years and the elements.

The sense of dread holding me in its clutches worsened. Since the incident in the library, Reggie had thrown all of her energy and focus into books from the secret collection. Roderick had been busy preparing for winter so I saw very little of him.

I felt very small in this fenced space, itchy all over, and like I was coming apart. I read the stones:

Beloved Father. Taken too soon.

Taken by what? Whatever genetic weakness marked the Usher bloodline?

Some of the smaller headstones had sculptures of lambs. It took a moment before I understood what I was looking at.

"Children!" I gasped.

* * *

In the house's unnerving stillness, I wandered into the kitchen, not sure what I was in search of. I opened cabinets. Cans of things that could have been there for decades filled whole sections of the pantry. One entire room contained dry and boxed goods and, mercifully, a shelf upon which numerous jars of instant coffee shared space with bags of tea. In the far corner of the kitchen, I found the metal door to the walk-in fridge and freezer. Inside the first section were bags of oranges, carrots, potatoes, and other hearty vegetables. The back end was filled with meats, enough for numerous winters for the three of us.

An entire cabinet contained powdered baby formula.

A DREAM WITHIN A DREAM

In one strange little cubby beside the kitchen door was a shelf for keys. The ones to my car hung from a hook in there alongside those for the estate's other vehicles. Another skeleton key dangled from a length of frayed ribbon.

I closed the cabinet only to return to it after I spied the door to the cellar in a dark corner at the very rear of the kitchen. Its ancient filigree knob was locked. I retrieved the skeleton key and was correct in my assumption that it was the one to the cellar door.

The door creaked open, releasing a smell my mind translated into the wet underside of a log mixed with cemetery earth.

Tombs, I thought and remembered what Reggie told me.

I stared down into the unlit abyss. Locating a switch, I flipped it up, and a bald yellow glow illuminated the space deep beneath a wooden staircase.

I'm not sure why I decided to go down there. Morbid curiosity, perhaps. I descended the steps, aware of the groan of the old wood beneath my weight, and of something else I couldn't identify until I was standing in the cellar under the house of the Ushers.

It vibrated through the dark rock walls, which glistened in spots with moisture. The tremor was everywhere and nowhere. It seemed to echo through the foundation and floor; the latter inlaid slabs in some places, bare dirt in others. As I listened, it resonated through my boots, into my teeth, my bones—even deeper into my soul. I realized it was the falls crashing down beside the house and infusing the air with mist, as they had for a time far longer than the existence of the estate upon their bank.

A necklace of bare bulbs lit my surroundings. I gazed around at a succession of corners, vaults, and hiding spaces. Some of the damp-swollen doors stood open, revealing broken furniture, old bicycles, and lumber that had almost melted into the floor. Farther along, where the air hung thick and clotted, I encountered car parts, a worktable, vice, and other tools. Past that marker, the way branched, and I realized the cellar ran the approximate length and width of the house. Always there was that thrum, that eternal reminder of the waterfalls.

I tried to imagine a crypt beneath the house—the very place where we lived— and the crushing madness born of grief that led to its creation. Only when I found myself staring at the entrance to that unthinkable place did I consider the possibility that I'd gotten lost and might never find my way back to the cellar stairs.

That place.

It had the feel and look of a sepulcher with cement slabs upon which caskets were laid. Three. The significance of that number didn't register until I saw that two of the caskets appeared very new, the other far older and there for years.

The brother's.

Hands shaking, I reached for the lid, whose polish had withered beneath the house and was coated in a mix of dirt, dampness, and cobwebs. Eyes wide, I envisioned the processions of past visitors to this somber place lit only by the dimmest reach of the line of old-fashioned naked bulbs. Those who'd lived and slept here before me ... their entire existence had been determined by two factors—being of the Usher line and this subterranean mausoleum through which a constant dirge played.

Those two other caskets.

"Reggie and Roderick," I sighed in sad realization. Preparation in case the Crimson extended its skeleton's touch past Usher House's outer walls. And, at least in Regina's case, should the curse within claim her first.

I blinked and came out of my trance. Revulsion filled me in equal doses for both the tomb I had discovered and also my willingness to search it out. I whirled, and the darkness extended its reach. The thrum of the falls pulsed at my ears along with my rising heartbeat. Out of the sepulcher, I found myself standing on dirt floor—I was sure I'd crossed concrete en route to the tomb. My panic built, a taste of the Usher's madness. A low, frightened mewl slipped up my throat and past my lips. In that moment, I sympathized with the long dead brother who howled at the full moon.

I made another turn—a wrong one—and guessed I'd arrived to some outer stretch of foundation that braced the nearby falls. The ground was wet. Water dripped from the stones. The thrum was double that anywhere else I'd been and pounded through the floor with an unpleasant slither.

Lost. I was lost.

A DREAM WITHIN A DREAM

The same calm I'd shown in Boston, shown before Boston and the Crimson, vanished. I turned and ran—

—right into the man who'd already saved me once, Roderick.

I called his name and embraced him.

"You shouldn't be down here," he admonished.

I pressed my head against the top of his chest, the fit beneath his neck ideal. Dare I think it? Perfect. Though clearly angry with me, he thawed enough to wrap an arm around my lower back while exhaling in frustration. The scent of his skin and clothes dispelled most of the fetor around us.

"Why?" he demanded. "What were you doing here?"

I looked up into his handsome expression and those wounded blue eyes. "I wanted to see it for myself. Reggie, she told me about the tomb."

"The tomb," he huffed.

Then, guiding me away from that part of the cellar, we returned beneath the chain of light bulbs and found our way out of the underworld. There were the stairs. Roderick had rescued me, and I was more relieved than I thought possible.

"Do you want coffee?" he asked after taking back the key and locking the cellar door.

I shook my head. He considered me, his frustration clear. But I didn't shrink beneath Roderick's gaze. No, I blossomed, loving his attention. He cracked a smile and shook his head, the expression more playful than disapproving.

"What am I gonna do with you?" Roderick asked.

I reached for his hand. "I have some ideas."

* * *

He led me to the base of the stairs. I looked higher. The worry returned to my face. "Reggie," I said.

He followed my gaze up to the landing and along its course in the direction of the Yellow Room. His throat, scruffy from not shaving, tightened under the influence of a heavy swallow. "This way," he said.

I followed him past the gym, through the long hallway that led to the dining room with its faded peacock wallpaper print, to a corner where an opened door cloaked the existence of another behind it. My heart resumed its gallop. That door led through a room where cartons were stacked to yet another, and there was the one the house's handyman claimed as his own.

It was a simple space, the big bed lacking a headboard, unmade, the rumpled covers showing the reverse bas-relief imprint of the body that slept there. A man's dresser. Piles of clothes on the floor in a corner waited to be washed, folded, and put away. Balled socks, boxer briefs, and a few T-shirts sat on top of the dresser from the last laundry day. The room smelled of Roderick—divine!

He seized me into his arms and crushed his lips over mine. In the dim light oozing past the curtains, I recorded details—the magnificence of his torso when his shirt fell, its perfection earned in the gym not far from his secret room; the skill in which he removed mine; the ease with which he carried me to his bed; and how the covers smelled of him.

His tongue pleasured me, and I swear my consciousness jumped out of my body to float above the bed with the joy being showed in the otherwise gloomy house of the Ushers. There, my mind wandered. This room, nestled where it was, surely hadn't been a bedroom in the days when Ushers filled the upstairs chambers—it was too near the dining room. And, thinking this, I placed its location in relationship to the cellar.

We were directly above the tomb, I was sure of it.

Roderick entered me, and that notion got tabled as my consciousness slammed back into my physical self. I gasped his name. Roderick growled in a deep animal's tone. I didn't have much to compare his skills with other than he was better—so much more gifted—than the few young men I'd known before him.

Given his artful lovemaking, I might have missed what I then saw. The dimming glow from beyond the windows conspired with my flesh to overlook certain details, but as he dominated above me, his powerful hands bracing the mattress and pinning me beneath him, I noticed scars above both of his wrists. Two jagged lines cut deep enough into his flesh to leave permanent marks.

A DREAM WITHIN A DREAM

My eyes shot open. I think he mistook my shock for ecstasy. There was that, too, crashing over me in icy-hot waves along with the realization that the man whose bed I shared was no handyman alone but the mad son of the family I'd been told had taken his life and was interred in the cellar tomb—

Roderick Derry Usher!

He powered onward. At one point, I sensed the vibration from the waterfalls again, echoing through the house, through him and into me. The falls were a permanent part of Roderick like the spores of mold drifting in from the cellar to infect every atom of the house with madness.

The thrum and the madness.

The thrum.

And the madness.

The thrum...

And the madness!

When he climaxed, the last son of the Ushers howled like a wolf, and I screamed.

* * *

I huddled in a fetal curl in one corner of Roderick's bed feeling cold and haunted. He sat on the edge of the mattress, his sweat cooling, a phantom conjured by the new night.

"I have to check in on Reggie," he said.

I nodded but couldn't locate my voice. Roderick stood and pulled on his discarded clothes and then left me alone on his bed with the terror of what I'd learned only starting to register.

* * *

Two days later, I slipped out of the house, my car keys in hand. The first snow fell— only a dusting. Nothing that would keep me from navigating the roads out of Usher

Falls and back onto Route 2. From there, I didn't know where I'd go, but I couldn't see that far yet, only the first part which meant escaping.

My car was where it was supposed to be in the circular drive but wouldn't start. Completely dead, I popped the hood, not knowing what to look for. But even the least knowledgeable rube at auto mechanics like me could see that the battery had been removed.

* * *

Why not tell me the truth at the start—that Roderick hadn't died years earlier and that he was really Reggie's brother?

Madness, my inner voice answered.

Why strand me here?

Madness.

I returned to my room and locked the door. Outside, the storm blustered, and all was white. I paced the room. *I'm trapped here. But why? It's more than the explanation of a safe house Reggie sold to me.* The day darkened. A knock sounded on the outside of the locked door.

"Helaine, dinner," Roderick said.

I told him I wasn't hungry, claiming to not feel well. An icy chill crept around the room. I built a fire. Eventually, with breathing no longer easy or involuntary, I crawled into the Blue Room's canopied bed and passed out more than slept.

At one point, I stirred, sure there was someone else in the room. I inched my eyes open. A skeletal figure hovered between the bed and fireplace clad in scraps, the thinning remains of blonde hair hanging from the crown of its skull. I froze. The skeleton observed and chuckled in Reggie's voice. Everything blurred. When I returned from the spell, the room was empty, the fire almost out.

* * *

We sat in the conservatory. I fixed a glare at Reggie without blinking. She held the guitar but it appeared to demand the last of her strength—that, at any moment, she'd lose her grip and the guitar would fall, striking the floor and unleashing a jarring, deafening echo off those empty walls.

"Why, Reggie?" I demanded.

She glanced up, seeming to locate me by voice rather than through sight. "Why what, Helaine? Why invite you here, safe from the Crimson?"

"Safe?" I repeated. "Roderick is …"

"My brother, yes."

"You told me he died—that he was buried in the cellar tomb!"

Reggie's chin sagged down to rest on her breast, which rose and fell with labored gasps for air. "Oh, yes, I did. It wasn't a lie so much as a retelling of the truth. You see, Helaine, Roderick did nearly succeed in taking his own life. Our father—you remember him and what a bore he could be—a bore and a tyrant! He was so enraged that he dragged my dear brother down there, where he'd had the workmen install a coffin, and he locked Roderick inside it. All to teach him a lesson. One about the importance of life. I fear my poor brother suffered more as a result of that parenting misstep. He hasn't exactly been right in the noggin since."

"You're mad—all of you!" I said.

Reggie laughed, the sound juicy and steeped in pain. "We're Ushers."

"You still haven't answered my question," I pressed.

"Why I invited you here? To give him—and this house—the one thing I couldn't."

She glanced up, a sharp little smile playing on lips that had gone blue. The smirk shorted out with a cough, and a cocktail of drool and blood sprayed the front of Reggie's satin robe. The guitar fell from her hands. The jostled sound lived up to my expectations. With eyes no longer able to blink, Reggie followed it inelegantly down to the floor.

"Roderick," I called.

And then I screamed his name.

* * *

I waited in my room, my breaths coming in shallow little sips like those Reggie had made in the conservatory—her last.

The proof of her death came in a loud animal's roar broadcast through the conservatory. Roderick's rage and sorrow echoed through the House of Usher, up through the tall ceilings, circle towers and turrets, and down the gallery stairs, through its vast ground floor, library, and dining room where no one ever gathered to break bread anymore; lower, deeper, into the dark and shadow-filled recesses of its cellar.

In its wake, an ominous stillness settled over the manor and its endless succession of rooms.

* * *

I waited for Roderick to seek me out. When he didn't, I went in search of him. I found him in the library. He stood on the same rolling ladder and was returning the poisonous texts to their locked shelf high above the others when I entered.

"She thought there might be an answer in the books," he said. "A way to cheat the Usher Curse, to cheat death. There wasn't."

He waited on the ladder, his expression frozen in a scowl. At that moment, I forgave his deception, his madness, and only remembered what I had loved about Roderick Derry. So handsome and tragic …

I reached for his hand, but he pulled away and shot me a menacing look. "Don't," he growled. "Don't you ever touch me again!"

He stalked off, leaving me alone with a million truths and fictions cloaked in the false twilight within the house. For three nights, Roderick's howls echoed through the vastness that had swallowed me whole.

* * *

I boldly approached the Yellow Room, not knowing but suspecting what I would find. The room had been turned upside down, the curtains torn from the windows, the chairs, tables, and other furniture tossed on their sides. What had to be a hundred pills were scattered across the floor.

His sister's death had driven Roderick even madder. I was trapped in the house with the last insane heir of the Usher family.

Slowly, not daring to blink, I made my way downstairs and to the kitchen, aware of the silence bottled within the house of the Ushers in a way I never had until that moment. Along with the shroud came a ribbon of icy air that slithered across the kitchen floor.

The floor!

Drops of clotted and drying blood led from the section of counter where the knife block and one blade soaked in crimson rested. I tracked the blood to the source of the cold: the open cellar door.

How long I stood at the threshold above the top stair I cannot say. All at once, I thawed, hastened down the stairs, and back into that underworld realm, headed for the one place, the only place, that mattered.

I entered the tomb. The iron tang of blood hung thickly in the air in equal doses with cellar mildew. In the poor light, I gleaned that the lid of the oldest of the three coffins was partially opened.

I didn't want to look.

No, I didn't.

Left no other choice, I opened the coffin's lid, and inside were two bodies. Roderick, before dying, clutched the corpse of his sister lovingly against him in his mutilated arms, and, seeing this, I, like the last of the Ushers, went mad, my descent into despair set against the endless dirge of the waterfalls.

* * *

Reggie's cell was unlocked. I found enough signal in one of the circle towers to call up what remained of the day's news. Cities burned. Crimson was everywhere.

"Do not believe what you've been told by those so-called government experts," an older blonde woman with insane eyes drawled in a southern accent.

"There is no Crimson—just a big lie forced upon Americans by those who seek to worship at the altar of science and deny our one true god!"

A last gasp crackpot, I killed the phone and pitched it against the nearest wall.

* * *

I doubled over and retched. Nausea flared in my gut. I vomited again.

The one thing she couldn't give him or the house—

"Another Usher, a new heir to the family name," I said.

Lightning pulsed around and within me, the flashes blinding but wholly in my mind. No storm had arrived to blast this cursed house apart down to the water and bedrock. It was only morning sickness, not the justice I desired.

* * *

I fixed coffee and savored it while I recorded on paper all that happened here should anyone come looking; should Crimson burn out or be vanquished by Usher Pharmaceuticals or any of the other forces desperately trying to bring the world back from the brink of the abyss.

All of it written down, yes.

Now, to find the courage to walk out there and jump. You see, it's gotten brutally cold these last few days, and if I wait much longer, the falls will freeze over and—

DEAREST BERENICE

I.

As night is to day, darkness to dawn, there exists the thinnest sliver of a meeting point between extremes that is tangible yet seldom noticed. This in-between is located where winter touches spring, the waking world the dreaming, and the contrasting pulses of love entwined with hatred.

My name is Eustus—the last name of my family irrelevant, though you'll no doubt read about it in the coming weeks as much of what happened at the estate travels around the world and paints me as a monster. Monster. That's what she said years ago during my boyhood spent near the beach in Carlisle, Maine.

"You're a little monster!" my late cousin, Lorianne, would accuse when other family members weren't listening.

My mother always referred to me as her angel. The truth existed somewhere in the middle of those two extremes.

* * *

My mother's love of books got passed down to me. In that house, she'd built an impressive library where hardcovers and paperback novels were arranged neatly on shelves and also stacked in messy piles on every surface. This study in contrasts, like the extremes already alluded to, created the perfect balance of austere duty and unapologetic fun. She never married my father, and I often suspected he wasn't whom she claimed—some free, wandering soul who'd summered in Carlisle and left at the end of the season none the wiser about me.

I never missed him. I always loved her.

Especially when she revealed that she'd given birth to me in the library, among so many great authors.

"I was reading," she told me one summer night while we both wandered that room in search of discovering a good book and neither of us in any hurry to depart. "And you decided it was time for your Chapter One."

"Who?" I pressed. "Who were you reading? Shakespeare? Hawthorne? Edgar Allan Poe?"

She glanced over to one of the many piles of paperbacks rising in small mountain ranges around our wonderful library, knowing the exact location and identity of each title and author among the deep strata. "No, a sappy romance novel by Jo Atkinson."

My mother held up the beloved paperback, *Love Never Lies*, and I knew then what book I would carry to my bedroom and devour as the night's hours before my tenth birthday passed in a blur.

* * *

My mother had money—a lot of it—which earned her an undeserved reputation among others in our family. Though rarely spoken of directly to her, I often caught the shards of their resentment within earshot of conversations I wasn't meant to hear and, sometimes, vitriol in its harshest form by my cousin Lorianne.

All of this was before I met Berenice.

* * *

A DREAM WITHIN A DREAM

Like a dream, I read that paperback novel, loving it from the first sentence–*That summer, Mirith learned that love never lies.*

The story was about a naïve young woman who finds that the charismatic man she thinks she is in love with is a liar and a cheat. Heartbroken, she meets a handsome if roguish fisherman in a beachside town not much different from that beyond my family's estate and experiences a second chance at passion, this time genuinely. The writing was okay—decent enough that the novel was published. But what made me fall in love with Mirith's travails was the knowledge that her story was mine—the tale of my birth among the books of our wonderful library.

I devoured half the novel before the knock sounded at my bedroom door.

"Eustus?" my mother asked in a voice almost not there.

I came out of the world within the pages. "Yes?"

She entered, her smile that was always there displayed, but it was superimposed over a frown. It was my first clue of the in-between that linked extremes.

"Time for bed," she said.

"But–"

"No arguing. You've got a busy day tomorrow."

She kissed the top of my head, took the book, and folded the top of the page with a dog's ear as a way to mark my place.

My busy day. I pouted.

"What's that look for?"

"Why can't it just be the two of us?"

My mother exhaled, clearly tired. She was exhausted a lot lately, but I didn't know she was ill. "Don't you want cake?"

"Cake with *you*," I stressed.

"Don't you want presents?"

I was a boy but one much older than my years. "I have presents, lots of them—you, the library, this book!"

I picked up the paperback. She returned it to my nightstand and fixed me with an understanding look. "Family duties," she said. "Try to enjoy your birthday party–just like I plan to do my best to get through seeing your uncle and his wife."

My Uncle Robert—her brother—and Linda, my aunt. They were my mother's bane. Mine came in the form of their daughter, nasty Lorianne.

"Promise?" she pleaded.

I nodded for her benefit. A comfortable May breeze drifted in past the sills in my room scented of the green returning to life outside the walls of our castle filled with books and mysteries and, above all, happiness.

Day, night. Smiles and frowns. Joy and despair.

The life I loved and the death I would come to know in this house.

* * *

I was awake on the morning of my birthday before dawn, anxious over the day's auspices and exited to read more of the novel. I switched on the lamp and bunched my pillow behind my back. The day surfaced from the darkness and, conscious of the dividing line, I stared past the window into the trees, my focus captured by the shift in those two realities.

It was the first time I consciously took notice of the in-between. Maybe it was a leaf on the red maple visible in the opening reach of daylight as the sun lifted over the Atlantic. Or it could have been the way the reading lamp embossed the window screen. I looked and was possessed, forgetting the book in my hands, where I was, and the early hour.

I came out of the fugue an untold time later with zero fanfare or prodding. When the long stare ended, I was rigid against the pillow and the room awash in the new day's brightness. My eyes stung from the glare. My limbs ached from maintaining their fixed position. Worse than any of it was my confusion.

The door opened and my mother glided in carrying clothes—jeans, a button-down shirt, and the new light sweater she'd ordered for my birthday with thick stripes of chocolate brown and jade green. She unfolded the sweater and presented it to me.

"Only until it warms up," she said, not noticing the dazed look of my expression.

A DREAM WITHIN A DREAM

She set the clothes on the foot of my captain's bed, the one with the shelves underneath I'd loved as a little boy, and glanced up.

"Eustus, is something wrong?"

"No," I lied.

* * *

The house. It was a grand palace perched on a rise and surrounded by stands of ancient trees. Built by my great grandfather, ownership had passed to my grandfather and then my mother, bypassing her older brother, Robert, who squandered his money and would have lost the house through one bad business gamble or another, according to the little my mother revealed.

Our rooms were on the ground floor at the back of the house and close to the library. Doors off the dining room led to a rear garden where heritage roses were in bloom from June to September. A trail pounded into the earth over the years cut through the dense stands of trees crowding in to surround the house and down to a private stretch of beach.

We ate a light breakfast of fresh fruit and hot tea—I'll always recall how good it tasted. A vast spread was planned for later and, as my mother promised, there would be cake.

* * *

Let me tell you about Lorianne.

Like my Uncle Robert, she was the first to be born in the next generation of our family. With that came a natural sense of entitlement. My mother legally and fully owned the family house and lands as well as a majority holding in the company that had provided for us so nicely. But her brother resented that she was chosen over him by their father, and through trickle-down genetics, I suffered as a result. From my earliest memory, Lorianne was a villain more sinister than any found in the pages of the books within our wonderful library.

When I was no more than three, she would push me down, often hit me when no one was watching, and when someone responded to my cries, she'd claim it was an accident, my fault. Not long after, she'd warn me not to tell.

"If you do, I'll come back at night and make sure it's even worse!" she'd threaten in a voice meant only for me.

Even then, her image struck me as unusually evil, and when I saw photographs of her when she was younger, a level of it radiated from her sharp smile, the dark ringlets of her curls, and, above all, her eyes. Those brown lenses contained malevolence from the start.

Lorianne was three years older than I. But we were both ancient souls—me with my books, she with her natural cruelty.

* * *

Car doors closed like thunderclaps on that vibrant May day set beneath cloudless blue sky the color of comfortable denim. Helium balloons lined the flagstone walk. People arrived: friends, cousins, relatives, others. Presents grew in piles atop the folding table covered with a paper cloth decorated in a colorful animal pattern. The caterers and wait staff prepared to make tray passes with deviled eggs, crab cakes, and other tasty bites. The cake was three layers and round—golden with chocolate frosting, doused in shredded coconut, and decorated in cherries. The big crystal punch bowl and matching cups were kept filled.

Their new car pulled into the driveway. I don't think I ever saw them drive the same vehicle twice. Out they stepped. My Uncle Robert, with his shock of silver hair, eyed the house with his usual mix of jealousy and disdain projected, my Aunt Linda, and the monster who'd labeled me one. She carried a gift bag with lots of blue tissue paper showing from the top. I wondered what it contained—a mousetrap ready to crunch down on finger bones the instant I slid my hand into it? A black widow spider? Acid?

The princess was dressed in a blue dress with white polka dots. My eyes drifted toward the pattern, and it happened again for the second time that day. I fell into the gravitational pull of the circles, and time lost all meaning.

A DREAM WITHIN A DREAM

When I woke from the spell, she was at my back, snickering in a low, mean whisper. "I think he's dead," Lorianne said. "Yes, either dead or staring off into space."

I wiped the drool from my mouth and attempted to hold onto the vision I'd glimpsed in that other place in-between. Her cackles sharpened. I moved away from the window where I'd drifted off and pushed past her.

As I did, she hissed, just loud enough for me to hear, "Monster."

* * *

I sought comfort in the one place it was guaranteed: our house's library. In a corner of that room was the antique camelback sofa with carved wings and clawed feet that looked ready to run away under its own power, two club chairs, and a big library desk. The desk was positioned in a cubby so that enough space existed between it and the nearest wall for a boy of ten to hide.

Outside, my birthday party continued without its guest of honor. Inside, I wiped my eyes and wondered what was happening to me. In the safety of that corner, I understood that only one of my feet was planted in this world, while the other had inched past reality to a land of mist and phantoms.

The scuffle of approaching steps sounded from the other end of the library. I stilled my sniffles and hid, thinking it was Lorianne come to continue her taunts. No, the pair sounded older, heavier. The library doors closed. I waited, my breath held.

"Will we do this every time you visit?" my mother asked.

I tracked her voice to the antique sofa and my uncle's to one of the club chairs.

"That's up to you," he said. "And I shouldn't have to visit this house. By rights, it's mine."

She sighed. "Are we going to go there again, too?"

Silence.

"How much do you need this time?" my mother asked.

"You could just roll the combination into the vault's lock and leave," he said.

She drew in a deep breath and just as deeply expelled it.

"The usual. Plus five thousand."

A jingle of keys followed. She stood and walked toward the desk. I made myself even smaller as she unlocked the drawer that contained an exquisite antique lacquered box wherein her checkbook and what she called her "mad money" were kept—a few thousand tucked away as a rainy day fund.

"You're not looking well," Uncle Robert said.

"Oh, I wonder why that is, *Brother,*" she fired back.

"Gloomy Maine winters. Try getting more sunlight. I hear Vitamin D does wonders."

She wrote out a check, her scribbles sounding fast, furious, and tore the check from the book. "Here."

He shifted, and I heard him draw out his wallet. "Pleasure doing business with you."

No further words were delivered. My mother again locked up the lacquered box and its treasures. At the library's door, my cousin Lorianne waited.

"What's wrong, Princess?" asked Uncle Robert.

In a voice that dripped with a sickening note of honey, she said, quite properly, "It's the birthday boy—we can't find him!"

My mother hastened past them and out of the library. In the hallway, she called my name.

Eventually, I snuck out of hiding and joined her.

"Where have you been?" she demanded.

"In my room. I came as soon as you called," I said.

My mother's harsh expression held for several more seconds—long enough for me to see that she wasn't well. She had aged between our breakfast of fruit and tea and the arrival of family. Then the scowl melted off her face, and she was the happy, free soul I knew and loved once again.

"Come on, my angel—let's join the party!"

She wore that smile on our way out through the open door, but I saw the anger and pain beneath it over the secret meeting I'd spied in our wonderful library.

DEAREST BERENICE

II.

Dearest Berenice.

My dearest Berenice.

Past and present. The sacred and the profane. Life's endings and death's beginnings.

I met Berenice in my second year in college, her first. I was studying Liberal Arts but had decided to pivot toward Mass Communications and English to earn my Library Sciences degree. The campus had a decent library—though, of course, I loved the one at my family's home more. I was seated at a carrel, my tablet turned off, an old hardbound book opened before me, when it happened again. I'd noticed the way the sunlight glinted off a section of varnished wall, and how it reminded me of something from home. A memory, not fully formed, projected onto that patch of wall. A summer day. A trip to the seashore. Only ...

And then I was gone.

A voice drifted in from the ocean. "Are you okay?"

An invisible bird flapped its small wings near my ear. I shuddered and came back from the place in-between realities. A figure leaned over the carrel, indistinct, a woman. Terror jolted me the rest of the way out of paralysis, for, in that moment, her eyes focused and I thought them Lorianne's. Dark, cruel, they stared without blinking. I gasped myself awake to see a lovely young woman watching me with obvious concern.

"I asked if you're all right. You were staring—"

"No, thinking," I corrected.

"You were thinking at me."

She smiled, and again, I suffered a terrible instant where past and present overlapped. The length of clean white teeth she flashed looked nowhere near as sharp as my cousin's. Just how pretty the girl was registered on the other side of my shock. She wore her dark hair short, which accentuated a slender face. I liked her beauty mark. She dressed in stylish clothes—an olive top with long sleeves that looped around her thumbs, yoga pants that seemed to love her body, and a messenger's bag, leather; likely Italian and well-traveled according to its wear. She smelled like lily of the valley in the perfect dose.

"I'm so sorry," I apologized. "When I get these deep thoughts, I go there. Really go there!"

We earned disapproving scowls from other students seated nearby in the campus library. The spotlight was back on me, as unwanted as during boyhood days spent in my cousin's dangerous company.

She flashed our new friends a look that inspired them to turn their attentions elsewhere. "That's right," she grumbled at the backs of their heads. Then, to me, she extended her hand. "I'm Berenice. If you're going to undress me with your eyes, we might as well get to know one another better."

I accepted her offer and shook. Now it was Berenice's turn to stare.

"What's your name?" she asked.

"Eustus."

"That's different. But I like it."

"I was named after my grandfather."

"You want to exit this snooze-fest and grab a coffee?"

A DREAM WITHIN A DREAM

"I don't drink coffee."

She tsked and made a face—another response particularly pretty.

"But I do like a good cup of tea."

* * *

We dated. One night, we did more and, somehow, it all seemed right, like two puzzle pieces from different boxes that somehow linked together seamlessly. Over those weeks at school, we got to know one another. Berenice had family—two parents and a sister named Lee. She wasn't close with any of them. She grew up in the Midwest, attended college in Maine on a full-ride scholarship. She loved all the famous dead male poets.

"You'd swoon over the wonderful library at my home," I said, unable to still my tongue.

"Library?" Her eyes widened, and again, I suffered a flashback to another year—that cruelest one when Lorianne roamed my family's house, ever there, always vicious and ready to make me bleed.

"Don't clam up," Berenice said, smacking the side of my bare leg.

An unexpected coldness drifted over my private dorm room. I'd revealed too much too soon. She already knew about the money and some of my family history—single mom, jealous relatives, and a glaring hole where my father's identity existed. It was part of the expected exchange of college lovers. But in mentioning the very heart of the story, I sensed I'd broken some unspoken but vital rule.

"First editions? Famous autographed copies?" she pressed.

I looked into Berenice's eyes and ordered my trepidations to wither. She wasn't Lorianne or anything like her. She loved books. We were an ideal match, different and yet connected like that dividing line between Night and Day.

"Yes, all those treasures exist within the library at my family home in Carlisle."

"I want to see—when can we go?" she said, the energy crackling off her flesh in tangible if invisible waves. "When, Eustus!"

"The house is closed up until the end of the semester," I said, which was the truth.

Berenice pouted. "But that's months away!"

In that instant, I slipped past lust and into love with Berenice. It wasn't that I planned or even wanted to, but her love of books became our link, our in-between.

When, later that very night, she asked me to marry her, I said yes. Not long after, we said, "I do."

* * *

We opted for a private ceremony, no family, just a few college friends. We held it at the gazebo in the park outside the school's library on a Saturday morning that dawned warm yet overcast—a taste of the last of April's showers and a preview of summers in Maine both at the same time.

Berenice wore a simple white peasant dress and lace veil and carried a bouquet of tulips picked in the park. I wore jeans. It was, all considered, quite perfect. Even the rain held off until after the vows. We celebrated with cupcakes and sparkling cider in the campus cafeteria. On the long drive up the coast to Carlisle, however, the storm's deluge hammered our car with a ferocity that was nearly blinding.

Boldly, I reached over and squeezed my new bride's knee. My dearest Berenice. My wife.

I'd had the house opened up, cleaned, and readied for a honeymoon enjoyed in our new home together by the sea. Most of that time, I expected, was to be spent in the wonderful library. We were in love. The worries that plagued me whenever I pondered returning to the home of my mother waned.

What was it I saw on the wall? That reflection of sunlight?

I choked down the memory. We were in the present not the past.

The rain let up with shocking quickness and cut out all at once. We traveled from its gloom into a swathe of afternoon sunlight and, once more, I thought about the extremes and the dividing line in-between that joined them. But that thought only briefly occupied my mind.

A DREAM WITHIN A DREAM

"Look!" Berenice exclaimed. "Oh, look! Pull over, Eustus! Please—pull over to the side of the road!"

From the periphery, I glimpsed what she saw, the source of her excitement. The rainbow formed a brilliant arch above the greening Maine countryside in vibrant bands of yellow, red, and amethyst edged in gray. A rainbow—the link between dark sky and clear. And, at that moment, I believed it a sign of hope and benevolence to mark our wedding day.

Honoring my new wife's request, I pulled over to the side of the interstate, where others had gathered to view the spectacle. Berenice jumped out of the car, her phone in hand, ready to snap pictures.

Pictures of the rainbow that the gods had sent to us in honor of our union.

I remained behind the wheel a moment longer, aware of my smile. I glanced at my reflection in the rearview for proof of that joy. Yes, I was happy—happier than I'd been since boyhood days and nights spent lost in the wonderful library.

From the side of my eye, I saw the car speeding at us, its driver later to admit he was distracted by the vision of the rainbow, that symbol of hope. Slick roads didn't help. He slammed on his brakes, clipped my fender, and went off the pavement, colliding with the beautiful young woman dressed in white taking photographs of the vast light in the sky.

My dearest Berenice.

* * *

My mother died at home. Still, how I hated hospitals.

I sat in a boxy room on an uncomfortable chair while the weather report ran muted on the flat-screen hanging off a metal arm bolted to the wall. Bright skies were promised now that the rain had swept out to sea.

Around me the pulse and hum of electronics fed my despair. My eyes wandered the cyanotic blue stripe of paint running across the beige wall halfway up and vanished. What could have been minutes or hours later—days—a nurse's voice summoned me back from in-between real time and dreamland.

"Sir, sir, can you hear me?"

I made the excuse that my grief had obliterated me. It was easy to believe, and she bought it. Even more so when the list of my new bride's injures was laid before me to digest. Lacerations and broken limbs were the least of Berenice's afflictions. She'd been intubated. Though tests were still being run, the emergency room doctors suspected traumatic brain damage. While being assessed and given live-saving care, she'd suffered a kind of epileptic fit. Berenice had yet to regain consciousness. There was plenty of doubt she ever would.

I made the call to her parents and identified myself. The hour was late. No good news ever arrives via phone calls after dark.

"Husband?" her father huffed.

"Sir, there's been an accident. Beren—"

"Who are you?"

"Berenice, she's been—"

"Annabelle, Lee—get in here. I'm putting this on speaker."

I told them what happened. Late the next day, my new wife's parents and younger sister Lee entered the corridor, their steps pounding a terrible staccato through the somber space of the Critical Care Unit. They saw me seated among the chairs and accidental garden formed by potted palms in the waiting area. I stood.

"Are you Eustus?" Berenice's father asked.

I nodded, and then he punched me hard enough to send me spilling across the floor.

* * *

There was more I wanted to tell them, but my bride's family was beyond hearing anything. To them, this visit to a Maine hospital was mere ceremony, a goodbye. They would grieve their Berenice while she yet lived in a possibly constant vegetative state. When Berenice died, they would not attend the funeral, I knew. They'd already buried her in her hospital bed.

I entered the room. The wheeze and tick of the machines maintaining a counterfeit version of life transported me back to that year, the end, when my mother's illness feasted and my Uncle Robert's family moved into the house. The mangled lump in the hospital bed no longer resembled the spirited young woman who had forced me to love her. Worse, when I inched my gaze up to the living corpse's face, I saw that her head trauma had done something to alter the shape of Berenice's skull. Swelling, no doubt—but it had coaxed open both of her eyes at sharp angles, and she stared at me ... not so much with a blank expression as one of malevolence.

Those dark eyes! How they cursed me—so much like my cousin Lorianne's in that lost and fragmented past.

This is the present, Eustus, my sane, inner voice attempted to remind me.

"No," I whispered. "This is the in-between place, for past and present are linked."

* * *

The doctor planned to transfer Berenice to a facility for long term care. They had done all that was possible for her.

"But she hasn't seen the library," I said.

"What?"

I shivered. The cold, white prison of my surroundings pressed in and down, readying to crush me, I was certain. "Doctor, I'd like to propose another solution and, as Berenice's husband..."

* * *

For the second time, the large downstairs bedroom near the library became a place of hospice. A special bed and all of the medical contraptions arrived. Then Berenice was wheeled in. I hired an around-the-clock nurse and extra staff to bathe and attend to her needs.

What's that?" asked the nurse. She indicated the wooden door in one corner of Berenice's room. "I went to hang my coat, thinking it was a closet."

I inched my gaze up and toward the false door to the vault. "That? A relic, nothing more."

When they had her settled, I retired to my old boyhood room with its captain's bed and grieved.

* * *

Darkness settled over the old house. In what was once my mother's sickroom and now my dearest Berenice's, oxygen hissed into lungs and machines fed an illusion of life into the shell of a body from which all spirit had already flown. The nurse kept vigil, checking vitals and recording numbers and values on the company-issued computer tablet always within reach. She drank cups of tea and water with ice. She played soft music on her phone for my wife, who was beyond hearing.

"You said she liked poetry," the nurse said.

"And poets."

"Perhaps she'd like me to read to her. Do you have any of her favorites?"

Our wonderful library contained the works of all of Berenice's favorites. I promised to fetch a volume or two and slipped farther down the hall to the vast room of books. The sweet vanilla smell of the stacks welcomed me in. I returned to the antique camelback sofa, which I'd recovered following their treachery the year I was seventeen, and sat. The comfort of the cushions welcomed me home like a hug. I wondered if the clawed feet would clack across the floor, the sofa at long last sprinting away and taking me with it.

I closed my eyes and resumed weeping. But my tears shorted out without warning like the rain on the afternoon of our wedding. I opened them, and my focus traveled into the stacks, where they remained locked for most of the rest of the night.

* * *

I came out of the fugue and left the library. Early morning broke outside the walls of the family house. All was steeped in thinning grayness. I splashed water on my face, fixed two cups of tea in the kitchen, and steeled myself for the next full day of this new and ugly normal.

Berenice was the victim, but she hadn't traveled to the abyss alone.

A DREAM WITHIN A DREAM

The respirations and pulses of the machines that both maintained and mocked her greeted me ahead of the terrible image when I made it to her sickroom and stared in through exhausted eyes. Berenice, flat on her back, was where I expected. But the nurse slumbering in the chair beside the hospital bed was not aware of one vital change in her patient's condition.

Berenice's eyes were opened and trained upon me, their expression accusing, hateful. Both mugs slipped from my shaking hands and shattered with twin thunderclaps upon the ancient hardwood floor; it wasn't my wife in that bed but Lorianne, returned from the grave!

DEAREST BERENICE

III.

Death and strangulation.
The past. The present.
Life and lifelessness.
In my teen years, my mother withered. She hid her decline the best she could until there was no avoiding the truth. We took to our wonderful library and lost whole days and nights reading, vanishing into fantastic worlds.

"Where, Mother?" I had asked before the mad spiral of days after my uncle and his family moved into our home under the pretence of caring for her through her final days. "Where in this room was I born?"

Her smile was a second late in arriving, proceeded by chagrin. I sensed she would lie—a pretty, improvised fib meant to charm. I wasn't wrong, and her ploy worked. "Why, Eustus, there—on that shelf, between the fabulous mythologies of the Greeks and the ones of their relatives far to the north, the Norse. And in the

A DREAM WITHIN A DREAM

bookcase that contains Jo Atkinson's novels of sweet love and triumph. Oh, and here, on this very antique sofa!"

"And my father?" I asked.

"Gone. Returned to the sea like in a Herman Melville tale. He never knew you, though if he had, he'd have loved you as much as I."

That last part was the truth. Never had I doubted my mother's love only her honesty. I gazed into her sad smile and knew I was seeing a ghost.

Not long after that occurred, a darkness fell over our home. The memory of that time will always stay fresh, a never-healing wound. Other shadows snuck in around the corners and through cracks and the space between atoms and molecules, and rooms that had always felt bright now brooded in a kind of apprehension—in anticipation. The wrongness revealed itself after my mother took to her sickbed and, more and more frequently, she stayed there.

The thunderclap of a car door's closing rocked the stillness. Another followed, and then a single knock on the front entrance.

I opened the door. My Uncle Robert stood outside in the October chill. Colored leaves detached from trees and quietly fluttered in a silent breeze, for the world seemed to hold its breath. My Aunt Linda and cousin Lorianne flanked him. All smiled ... and oh, the sharpness of their expressions!

"We're here to help," I heard him tell her.

"No," my mother protested from her bed. "I want you out of this house—now!" Her voice rose to a shriek only to sputter in yet one more coughing fit.

"Relax, save your energy. Sis, we've got everything covered. You just try to rest."

The shadows in the room solidified and crept up behind me. I whirled, and Lorianne stood within reach, her eyes wild, her mouth twisted in a lunatic's grin.

"You're mother's an ungrateful bitch," she spat.

Rage powered up from my chest. I made a fist and readied to strike her, but ceiling and floor exchanged positions as pain exploded across the right side of my face. She'd lashed out at me faster and with greater efficiency, continuing what I already knew: my cousin was a predator and she considered me easy prey.

"You're not in control," she growled over me in a low voice. "And you'd better remember that I could kill you anytime I wanted. I almost did once before. And you ... it would be so easy, and nobody would care, you little monster!"

She made another lunge at me. I scrambled away, putting enough distance between us, and involuntarily waved a flag of surrender.

For the next seven months they took control over our home, and I became my cousin's constant victim.

* * *

I went back to school, and my grades suffered. My teachers assumed this fact owed to my mother's dwindling health, and they were partially correct.

Over the course of that hellish winter trapped inside the walls with them, I noticed things went missing—the exquisite Smithfield credenza in the dining room, the Red Willow china and, one afternoon, when I returned to the house from the school bus, the antique sofa in the library. Before that day, I'd noted that our home had taken on a disheveled state, with things touched and examined but not put back in the pristine order my mother and I had maintained in every room save the library throughout happier years. I knew they were ransacking the place, assessing what was valuable, then selling off pieces. More than once I caught Uncle Robert strong-arming my mother for the combination to the vault.

When she refused to be bullied, he growled, "When you're dead, I'll cut that door off with a blowtorch and everything inside will be mine anyway!"

To this, she'd laughed. "You will never possess what's inside there. My fortune belongs to my son."

"Your son? Not until he's eighteen, Sis, and a lot can happen over the next three months."

She didn't respond, and at that instant the February cold swirling outside the house's sturdy walls snuck past the windows and filled me.

They're going to kill me, I thought and knew it was true.

* * *

A DREAM WITHIN A DREAM

As had become ceremony, a dark form of ritual unseen by any save the four who performed it, I was summoned for dinner, which my aunt had prepared. My uncle sat at the head of the table as he always did as though he owned the place. Aunt Linda was seated to his left, a fresh, expensive bottle of wine opened, her glass half emptied of its contents before one bite of dinner was consumed. Their cruel princess sat across from me. I didn't want to eat.

"So how was everyone's day?" my aunt asked.

I was a prisoner in a cell with no bars, my mother more so, and my aunt seemed oblivious to these facts though surely she was just as culpable as the other two criminals.

I didn't answer. Uncle Robert reached for the platter containing the roast and carved it. The meat was beyond rare. Blood flowed. My nausea built.

"I had a great day," Lorianne declared.

"Why's that, Princess?"

"I'm going to start a dance studio here—I've found the perfect space," she said, eyeing me with one of her cutting glances, the white teeth she bared those of a vampire in my imagination.

I didn't ask for details. There were enough rooms in the house, and anything that occupied her attention meant less focus on me. My mind was stuck in a loop. *They're going to kill me—with my mother gone, everything will be theirs!*

"Eustus?" my uncle prodded. He held the platter of meat out toward me. I came back, saw all of the blood leaking from the slices, and nearly retched.

"No, thank you. I'm not hungry," I said and rose from my chair.

The malevolent smile on my uncle's face persisted. "Sit. You haven't been excused."

"May I—"

"No. Your aunt has gone to a lot of trouble to fix dinner. The least you can do is show some respect."

I sat and choked down enough to satisfy him.

How we got on the subject of heroes eluded me. Their voices degenerated into a stinging, white noise whine as the clocks in the house slowed, and time dragged out.

"Eustus?" my uncle asked.

All eyes were upon me. "Yes?"

"Heroes—who are yours?"

I wanted to reference a dozen—a hundred—authors celebrated within the walls of the library.

"My father," I said, "who left to go to sea, who fought dragons and rescued maidens and whom the gods smiled down upon. A great man, he never wanted temples built in his honor, and so he made sure I didn't know him."

Silence filled the room, and no one spoke or asked my opinion after that.

* * *

They watched, always watched me, and so I waited until a late hour when they slept upstairs before creeping into my mother's sickroom. There, the frail form on the bed barely showed proof of life. We were close to the end, I sensed. Holding in my misery, I woke her. "Mother," I whispered.

She jolted, and terror filled her eyes—whether for unwanted houseguests or the specter of Death, I couldn't tell. Not that it mattered. In the wan glow of the lamp always left on, she recognized me and relaxed. "Eustus."

I took her hand and kissed it. "Tell me, Mother."

"Anything."

"Do you promise?"

Worry inched back into her eyes. But time was short and truth demanded. She nodded.

"My father," I said. "What dark secret has Uncle Robert held over your head for so many years?"

Our eyes locked. There was no avoiding the answer any longer.

"Uncle Robert is your father," she said. "That wife of his, your true mother. And the cousin, that evil girl, is your sister, Eustus."

I listened, stunned, as she revealed a truth I no longer wanted.

"When you were born, Lorianne hurt you. She refused to share in her parents' attention. They worried she would kill you, and so you were to have been put up for adoption. But I loved you from the moment I first saw you, as did your grandfather, Eustus. I pleaded with my brother to let me adopt you, and he did. Our father was so horrified with Robert's behavior that he disowned him, threw him out of this house, and cut him off from making any decisions for the family business. But you ... you were innocent, an angel. My angel."

I thought about the story of my birth in the library: a lie, though not really. In there, I'd become her son surrounded by books and was loved from the beginning. The truth made me despise them more and love my mother to double what already was in my heart.

"On your birthday—when you turn eighteen—the house and all our holdings will be yours," she said before another coughing spell gripped her. "Be careful until you can have them safely removed. And tell me, please, that you forgive me, my son."

When the fit passed, I hugged her. It was like embracing fog, for she was almost invisible, almost gone.

"There's nothing to forgive, Mother. I owe you my life and every happiness I've known until this moment."

I didn't tell her what I suspected about them planning to murder me after she was dead. I understood that she already got that by the way she clutched me against her withering form.

* * *

I hated them—the aunt and uncle who were really my birth parents and, more so, the cruel cousin who was my sister. My mother's explanation made insane sense. Lorianne taunting me in my earliest memories. To her, I was a monster, unwanted in the paradigm of her family. But they were the true monsters to have treated me so, to have denied me protection. They would never be my family.

Sleep eluded me. The waking world was no clearer. At one point in that long night, I gazed at the wall above my bed and slipped past consciousness into the spell that was both curse and blessing.

* * *

"He's gone again," she said, punctuating the statement with a throaty chuckle. My cousin's—sister's—hated face materialized in the space before my eyes. "Maybe this time, he'll stop breathing and do our job for us!"

I tried to hold on to the territory where I'd traveled longer—in it, the blank patch of wall had become a window gazing out on a fantastic vista of ancient Greek ruins. Among the columns and carvings was an amphitheater, and in it my mother performed scenes reenacted from the greatest comedies and tragedies ever written.

The grandeur faded, and a demon from the modern world loomed over me. As I came to fully, she drew back and struck my face hard enough to knock me onto the floor.

"Wake up!" Lorianne shouted. And then she laughed.

* * *

Winter ended. Spring bloomed. The date of my eighteenth birthday neared. My mother's skin yellowed.

I returned from school that first week of May aware of an undercurrent in the house. My heart remained in a constant gallop. Whatever they planned would happen soon.

In the front hallway, books were strewn and stacked in heaps. As I watched, horrified, Lorianne emerged from the direction of the library, more volumes in hand. Not seeing me at first, she thoughtlessly tossed them down. My horror shorted out. Rage replaced it.

"Stop!" I bellowed.

She saw me and wiped her hands together as though to clean them of an unwanted residue at having handled the books. Her sharp grin returned. "You're home."

"What do you think you're doing?"

"I told you—creating a dance studio."

"What?"

"I've found the perfect space in that room of moldy books."

I shook my head. "No."

A DREAM WITHIN A DREAM

Her smile evaporated. "Yes, and don't even think for a second I won't get what I want. As for this," she spat, casting a look at the books, "they'll make for a great bonfire now that winter's over!"

She turned and marched away back to our wonderful library, her cackles echoing through the house.

They planned to murder me in the physical sense. Before that happened, Lorianne would kill my soul. The books ... my mother's and my beloved books!

I pursued her into the library, where whole shelves had been emptied. At that moment, I was forced to be even craftier than those who had invaded our home.

"Lorianne," I calmly said.

She tossed hardcovers into a pile on the floor. "What, monster?"

"Stop this, please."

"No."

"Stop and I'll give you what your father wants most."

She turned and eyed me. "What do you mean?"

"The vault—I'll open it for you. You can have everything inside if you'll just leave this one room and its books alone."

All of the confidence drained from her expression. "The vault?"

I nodded.

"I thought you didn't know the combination."

"I do. If you swear."

"I swear," she answered quickly.

Her word wasn't any better than her soul, I knew this. Still, obviously believing herself victorious, she forced me out of the library and into the sickroom, where my mother neared death with each hour. I heard the moans from the bed, sad as a scared kitten's, while turning the wheel, lining up the combination, and opening the heavy metal door to my most hated of enemies.

The lock released. I pulled on the door. The vault resisted. I yanked with greater effort and the door moved.

I knew what the vault contained—a fortune in gold, jewelry, stock certificates, and banded money, all of it lined up neatly on shelves. The stagnant breath of the air bottled long ago inside gusted out. Fresh air and light swept into the treasure trove, which was the size and depth of a coat closet.

Lorianne shoved me out of the way and entered. From the cut of my eye, I noticed sunlight on the patch of dark, varnished wall—a reflection off gold bars or any number of exquisite jewels. The urge to focus, to stare, briefly possessed me. For the next second, I felt myself drawn toward the dapples. But if I did, if I gave in, my advantage would be lost.

Not now, Eustus! my inner voice shouted.

I shook off the spell and threw all of my weight against the vault door. The door slammed shut. I spun the wheel.

Whatever effort she made to escape barely sounded through the metal.

"Yes, sister, I am a monster, I learned that from you," I said.

Sealing the wooden door over the vault's, I began to laugh in a low, throaty tone and imagined the grin on my face as looking quite sharp.

DEAREST BERENICE

IV.

Beginnings. Endings.

And what exists in the dividing line between extremes.

Like my mother, my dearest Berenice took to that room to die while those around her held vigil. A few cherished poetry books appeared on the nightstand alongside the hospice nurse's tools—salves, stethoscope, a kit containing razored scalpels and tubing—and I did my best to avoid looking in the corner where the fake closet door existed, the scene of my crime and also my one true victory.

Lorianne and what happened here was part of a different time, a life that was over.

Or so I believed.

* * *

On a warm, sunny May morning while the body of my new bride continued to live solely due to the machines attached to her like the strings of a marionette, I exited the house and ambled down the path beyond the overgrown back garden. The winter had brought down several trees—future work for the landscaper to attend to. But as I picked my way past the jagged remains of a sap pine, a quiet flutter of black teased my vision. I gazed in the direction of the Atlantic, still barely visible through the forest that had grown in to form a living wall, and the shadow slipped out of focus.

GREGORY L. NORRIS

Gooseflesh prickled across my arms despite the comfortable temperature and my long-sleeve shirt. I stared after the phantom no longer there. When I came out of this fugue, the sun had changed position in the sky; hours had passed.

* * *

It happened more frequently, those journeys in-between and the spectral visitations from whatever apparition haunted my family's home. I would curl upon the antique sofa in the library, which I'd recovered along with most, though not all, of the heirlooms sold off by those despised interlopers, and catch movement from the corner of my eye at the door or past a window. Then, turning to face it directly, see that the ghost had slipped past my attempt to identify it.

But when I entered Berenice's sickroom, which I did less as May crept onward, her eyes were always there, staring, accusing. It was as if she knew fully what I had done in that room four Mays earlier.

And that, even knowing why I did it, she didn't sympathize. I was a monster—and oh, how, if I looked quickly, the body in the bed had become Lorianne's.

* * *

I was born in this library after a fashion and vowed that I would die here among the greats. Birth and Death. If there was a birth cord, mustn't there also be a death cord? The life lived between them was the link, the connection that joined these extremes.

I woke in the darkness of the library unsure of where I was or even if I was. Had I died? And yet, I still drew breath. I located the lamp on the table beside the sofa and switched it on. Reassurance embraced me. I was within the familiar fortress of literature my mother had built and I'd added to over the past few years.

A smile tempted my lips, but my next thought removed it. That paperback—the one she read when I was born. Or, as was the actual case, the night they gave me to her. *Love Never Lies* ... only it had. My entire history leading up to my eighteenth birthday had been fabricated.

A DREAM WITHIN A DREAM

Berenice was dying not far away. We'd been in love, and she'd been stolen from me. Life—as cruel in some instances as kind in others. Those two extremes could drive a man to madness.

I scanned the piles of paperbacks, which I'd returned from the front hallway on that other May day, but couldn't find the novel. As the outside world surfaced with the rising sun, I realized I'd spent the entire night looking but with nothing to show for the effort.

* * *

My birth story a lie. The book gone. I wondered if I was really the corpse in the bed hanging on via life support.

My mind wandered to someplace other, the avenue there made possible by a skein of cobweb on the ceiling stirred by the balmy May breeze spiriting in past the open window. In a daze, I floated through the sunshine and down to the shore. Waves crashed across the rocky headlands. A lone figure dressed in black neared on the strip of beach last visited on a day four years earlier. The breeze caught in the folds of a funeral veil. The figure, a woman, held a paperback novel in her hand.

A chill engulfed me. She chuckled, the sound throaty. The temperature around me plummeted. I wanted to back away and leave, but the spell held fast. Then the woman turned, lifted her veil, and I was staring at Lorianne.

Her smile, so sharp—and those white teeth! Worse of all were her eyes, all pupil, all deep brown shadow.

"What?" I gasped.

She held the book of my birth in her taloned fingers. From the periphery, the romance novel was a baby.

"What are you doing here?" I demanded after locating my voice.

"You mean how did I escape from the trap where you entombed me?" she countered in a desiccated voice that scattered dust from her mouth. "I got out, and I'm always watching you, Monster."

The malevolent grin dropped from her lips. I blinked, and a mummified corpse swathed in rags occupied the space. The novel in its skeleton hand came apart in a shower of confetti. The wind carried the remains out to sea. I screamed myself awake.

* * *

That other day, after the vault door locked into place and I accepted what I would be forced to live with going forward, the rest played out with shocking clarity. What I needed to do. What I did.

It was to my benefit that neither *Uncle* Robert nor *Aunt* Linda were at the house, only their princess left to watch over and care for my failing mother's needs. They were out selling more family treasures I would mostly recover in the weeks that followed. Not fully knowing this, but aware my time was short, I grabbed a pair of Lorianne's sandals from her room and a bath towel. I stretched the towel out across the beach and arranged her shoes along with a water bottle whose contents I'd half poured out while hastening along the path.

It was enough and worked.

"Have you seen your cousin?" Uncle Robert asked after they returned from whatever dirty dealings took them into town.

I was in my mother's room pretending to do homework and keeping watch over the jaundiced, dying body he barely regarded through narrowed eyes.

"Said she was going for a swim," I lied.

"Swimming? Where?"

"The private beach."

"When?"

I shrugged. "About an hour ago, maybe more."

He shot a look out the nearest window. The sun was setting. But as my panic built, I wondered if he had heard it too—the telltale sounds of her fists as Lorianne hammered the thick metal on the other side of the vault door. That pounding ... surely he recognized it as clearly as I did. Only after he left my mother's sickroom did I realize I was hearing the mad pulse of my own heartbeats.

My eyes tracked his steps in the direction of the rear garden. Several long moments later, I heard his shouts as they carried across the estate.

A DREAM WITHIN A DREAM

"Lorianne! Lorianne!"

A smirk tempted my face. What I'd hoped for played out as I'd envisioned. The assumption was that the riptide had latched hold of his precious princess and dragged her out to sea. In the crippling quiet that followed, my uncle lost his taste for murder and rarely left his bed.

* * *

On the morning of my eighteenth birthday, I summoned the police to my home. A bold move, yes, given my own crime. But nobody knew that save me and one other, and, after presumed drowned for two weeks, she wasn't in any position to expose me.

"I want these trespassers gone from my home," I said. And then, to my uncle—my father—I growled the words in a threatening tone, "Get out of our house!"

Not an hour after they were vanquished, on the day of my birth, my mother took her final breath.

* * *

My dearest Berenice ... what made me think we could enjoy a happy life together in this place with its secrets and sufferings? Knowing that in my mother's old sickroom— now my wife's—my sins were imprisoned behind one false door and another made of impenetrable steel?

Lorianne's corpse was still in there mummified among diamond necklaces and sapphire rings, thick piles of hundred-dollar bills held together with brown paper bands, and stock certificates. I had created a tomb as cursed as any in Ancient Egypt's Valley of the Kings within the walls of this house. I'd had good reason, I told myself. Until now, I'd believed it. Ends justified by means. A defense against an attack.

A blight, now indelible, infected this house where love once lived but never would again. Gone were those wonderful instances when I traveled past the physical means and through whatever cosmic apparatus joined Reality with Fantasy, Morning with Dusk, Endings to Beginnings.

No more, the glances I'd taken into worlds of the Past and the Future. There was only Lorianne now, always waiting to further terrify and taunt me.

"When I first saw you in that hospital incubator, I thought you were the ugliest thing ever born," she said while half hidden behind the camelback sofa whose claws were dug into the floor in fear of her. "I thought, how hideous ... I'll do the world a favor in destroying it."

"If you wanted a glimpse at the truly ugly, you only needed to seek out the nearest mirror."

"What do you think I am?" she chuckled.

The sofa trembled, mewled in fright, and readied to run. I blinked, and it was me lurking behind the furniture. I had Lorianne's maniac eyes. I blinked again, and the rabid creature with bloodlust in its insane gaze was my dearest Berenice.

* * *

Those times when my consciousness left my body ...

On one of those final nights before what I did, it struck me that they were likely the result of Lorianne's abuse during the earliest moments of my life. When, as my mother revealed, my sister attempted to kill me. A bruise to my infant's brain behind the barely formed and flimsy protection of my skull. Hematoma. Traumatic brain injury. Personality Change. Monster.

I couldn't tell if I was dreaming or awake, alive or dead. Staring at the door to Berenice's sickroom, I looked to the face of the breathing corpse and saw those eyes opened and fixed upon me, hating me in silence.

Lorianne had escaped her tomb. Still questioning if I was in Reality or Fantasy, I closed the bedroom door and bolted it. Willing my legs to obey, I plodded to the closet. Two suns hung in the sky outside the nearest window. I pinched my eyes and saw that the second was a reflection cast by the first off the varnished wood of the wall.

Wake up, my inner voice pleaded. *Stop, Eustus—stop this before it's too late!*

Too late? It already was.

A DREAM WITHIN A DREAM

I opened the wooden door and turned the wheel. My pulse upped its tempo. On the last turn I felt the tremble as the lock released. Yes, I expected the vault to fly open, the hand on the other side pushing in desperation for air and escape and sustenance long overdue. But none of that happened, and the seconds drew out, becoming more like minutes.

Hands shaking, I reached for the handle and pulled. The vault door resisted. I tugged harder. The door complained but inched open. One more yank and it swung out, releasing the foulest blast of stagnant air into Berenice's sickroom.

A low, throaty chuckle sounded from behind me. I spun to see Berenice gone and Lorianne now upon the bed, fighting against the tubes and wires that held her restrained.

No, I've released her! All along, this was her plan! I fell into her trap, the voice inside me screamed.

Nothing after that was clear. Not the pounding on the door by the nurse. Not the interior of the vault as I tipped my gaze into its dark and damning maw.

* * *

The screams woke me. I came back to consciousness in the library—our wonderful library that my mother and I had so loved. Jolted, I sat up on the sofa aware of the wrongness in a way even more effective than the nurse's screams.

On the table beside the lamp I noticed my mother's beloved lacquered box, the one in which she'd once stored her checkbook and mad money. I hadn't seen the piece since before she'd taken to her sick bed and they'd invaded our house—it had gone into the vault for protection.

Fear rose up from my gut, infecting the rest of me. A low, throaty moan accompanied the growing emotion. I sounded like the scared sofa in my vision.

"Oh my God—look. *Look!*" the nurse screamed, presumably to the hospice worker who bathed Berenice.

Another scream joined the first.

"And in there, in the closet—look what's inside!"

I reached for the lacquered box. At the last instant, it spilled from my fingers and shattered across the floor, spilling its grotesque contents. Laid out from inside were stacks of money soaked in gore, the bloody scalpel taken from the nurse's supplies, and two eyeballs carved from their sockets. And, having landed upright, they stared at me without blinking, frozen with an emotion that could only be the purest hatred.

THE RED DEATH MASK

He'd never served in the military, never fought overseas against the godless mongrels of mud countries far from the shores of the U.S. of A. He hadn't gone into physical battle since his early teen years, when Heaven hadn't helped any of the boys or their families that had attempted to crush Tom Prince—she'd made sure that what was left over didn't remain standing or in town for long after she was done with them. Tom hadn't flown in choppers or wielded a rifle, but the camouflage battle dress uniform and steel-toe boots fit his athletic and commanding body as though they loved him. Riding three vehicles back in the convoy, he could have been a colonel. No, a general in charge of his troops. His bearing was, she often told him, equal to that of a god.

Marjorie Prince studied her son and smiled as the transport's tires beat tribal war songs over the pavement and their target appeared in the glow cast by the headlights, visible beyond the windshield. At that moment, she knew for certain she'd done more than raise a preacher man of first-rate charisma and influence. She had given birth to a second coming.

"Gentlemen, there's your objective," Tom drawled, his voice audible over the radio's chatter, the gunned engines, and the distant boom that could have been thunder from what promised to be an end-of-summer soaker or one more explosion as yet another layer of the old world vanished.

Marjorie's heart rate upped its tempo. The sharp little smile, displayed out of sight as all those around her focused on their mission, owed as much to the destruction as the resurrection she had made possible. While the Crimson raged and cities across the globe burned, a new beginning was taking shape, one clearer in design with each new fire and group death. And there had already been so many.

The lights were still on at the Usher Pharmaceuticals plant, the big sign a beacon in electric blue urging the convoy forward. With power grids failing, she assumed UP was running under its own generators like the Holy Lamb of Prospero Church. The most recent report between Usher and what remained of the former government showed promising results. They were close to cracking Crimson. Too close to having a workable defense against the plague and its variant mutations. And that could not be permitted under her, her son's, design for what was to follow.

The first drops of this latest summer storm struck the windshield. Marjorie licked her lips, aware of the sudden dryness that had desiccated her mouth. Between blinks, she was back there again in that shitty town, moving between her son, the future preacher, and any number of bigger, stronger boys. She saw Then-Marjorie draw back and swing, smacking faces hard across cheeks with the fullness of her palm, once enough to conjure blood from a shattered nose. The rest played out in fast forward—how she'd poisoned one offender's dog, a trusting golden retriever with a blue kerchief tied to its collar. How she'd schemed to seduce a different boy's father, which had been easy enough given her legs and the red dress she'd purchased for the task. The money to stay silent that came after. The accusation that another had fondled her boy—Tom was so convincing that every mark had paid well in one method or another.

All that came before was practice for now, when the Crimson raged across the planet and what had been was surrendering to what was soon to be.

Enough practice so she knew they'd get this right.

The transport jolted to a stop. Figures moved beyond the windshield and the rain began as soldiers in the two vehicles ahead of theirs streamed out, weapons drawn. Those around her waited an appropriate sum of long seconds—plenty of time to get the Judas goats ahead to attract, catch, and neutralize any danger from whatever defenses guarded the facility. The pounding of weapon's fire and angry voices clawed through the throbbing tenseness. Marjorie again licked her lips.

"All right, let's move out!" Tom commanded, his deep voice like a sermon.

A DREAM WITHIN A DREAM

Holding his pistol in one hand, he opened the door. Raw, damp air billowed into the transport smelling of the summer's heat and, at the edges, her son's cologne. He jumped free of their ride, his actions graceful, demanding notice. The storm soaked his expensive haircut and added a layer of wildness to his handsome face. Those blue eyes, now bluer in the light of the facility's sign, greeted Marjorie's. She smiled, nodded, and he offered a curt but resolute tip of his chin in response.

The last soldier out closed the door. Marjorie waited, holding her breath, and didn't expel it until the first explosion signaled that their team had breached the facility. More detonations tore through the maelstrom, the next round punctuated by the crash of shattered glass and more than a few screams. She grinned at the latter too—it wasn't as though the people working on a solution for Usher Pharm were desirable in the new order. It wasn't like they were real people, only wastes of oxygen and limited resources.

Immigrants likely, she thought and tsked. Liberals with their far-left agendas. The kind of nonbelievers in the Divine who'd paraded around in masks as though proud of that fact, flaunting the government's mandated infringements on American rights. *Let them burn,* she thought. *If the Crimson didn't get them, let them all burn now!*

Another explosion more powerful than the previous few rocked the night. This one culminated in a towering fireball that rose above the gutted main building. When the shockwave passed, Marjorie leaned closer to the nearest window for a better look. Most of the facility was on fire.

Beautiful, she thought.

Rain hammered the darkening battlefield. Through the window and deluge, Marjorie watched as their soldiers lined up the godless in the parking lot while the Usher Pharm plant burned, and how satisfying the pop of executioners' gunfire sounded. Even more so when one of the heathens attempted to escape.

That smile fixed on her lips, she settled back and waited, silently singing hosannas in the highest in the red haze of her thoughts.

The transport's door opened. Soldiers filed in, smelling of the rain and smoke. More narcotic was the scent carrying off the athletic physique of their leader, their god. Tom jumped in, soaked through from the storm. Marjorie's gaze locked with his. At first, she didn't see the blood, but she smelled it upon him and, for a horrifying instant, she feared he was infected. The telltale sight of blood on his unshaved right cheek—it was the mark of the Crimson, which opened lesions in the epidermis and poured forth in evidence of the Red Death churning deeper, the rot. It was in her son, which meant, at such close proximity, it was now also inside her, inhaled as she drank down the scent of his masculine sweat. The Crimson, latching onto her lungs with its tiny teeth, eating its way into her bloodstream, where it would grow, spread, feast—and, eventually, singing its own version of hallelujah to whatever dark god the disease worshipped, spill forth from her dying flesh on a deluge of red.

But no. The stain on Tom Prince's face was from one of the many blood sacrifices made to him on that night when everything changed and the last rule of the old world unraveled. New blood spilled for the holy lamb that would lead the world out of darkness.

At least control what was left of it when the Crimson burned out and the dust settled.

* * *

Crimson raged across continents. Mask mandates would have helped some, would have slowed it, giving scientists a chance to develop a cure, had so simple a solution not become a cause for war. Various biotech labs working in Germany, Buenos Aires, and Canberra all claimed progress in the fight against the plague, though none got so near to an effective vaccine as Usher Pharmaceuticals in the U.S. until a paramilitary operation destroyed research and prototype modified-RNA samples before they could be shared.

Phone service, already failing, went silent. The power grid suffered permanent interruptions, and skylines went dark. Fires raged, their hunger unable to be extinguished, and blood flowed both from the Crimson and due to the hands of men.

This was how the world died.

* * *

A DREAM WITHIN A DREAM

Another raid secured seven gasoline tankers. The convoy, guarded over by their ruler who again wore the military uniform he hadn't earned in service to a lost country, sped down Interstate 82 and through the picked-clean remains of Prospero and the surrounding towns. A few smaller fires burned nearby, but nothing that would affect their stronghold. Above it all, the steeple of the Holy Lamb pointed skyward out of respect while casting its giant middle finger at the surrounding firmament.

The usual rabble waited outside the sealed gates—beggars seeking entrance or at least mercy. Tom reached for the mic that connected him to the main guard shack and, on this morning, decided to show the intruders a measure of kindness. The two guards fired one warning shot each over the heads of those assembled, which got them moving. Those that lingered wouldn't be extended further goodwill.

The structure appeared ahead of them, situated alone and surrounded by former parking lots and concrete garages that could accommodate thousands of cars and plenty of buses. Now, the necessities for their survival occupied those spaces—refrigerator trucks, storage vans, military vehicles, and, soon, the tankers. Above all rose the mega-church with its seven stained glass panes, steeple, and network of phone towers and dishes that still linked them to functioning satellites in orbit around the infected Earth.

* * *

"... an evil born of man's secular approach to a godless lifestyle. First, A.I.D.S. warned of the homosexuals' abhorrent sins. Did we heed the message? **No!** Instead, a liberal government with an agenda and its puppet court system allowed men to marry other men." Marjorie shook her head and sighed for effect. "Play with brimstone, listeners, and I guarantee you that you'll get burned. Those in charge of the old world—pandering to homosexuals, shaking hands with the godless heathens overseas while waging war on religious doctrine here at home ... hell, they fought a war against Christmas! Is it any wonder this death has now consumed their world? But all is not lost. If you hear me, take hope for a last light of the world still shines—and shines brightly! Pastor Tom Prince loves you. Believe in him and what he represents and you will prevail through the dark days ahead.

"Do not believe what you have been told by those so-called government experts. There is no Crimson—just a big lie forced upon Americans by those who seek to worship at the altar of science and deny our one true god!"

She switched off the green button on her tablet.

"Until tomorrow," Marjorie whispered to the empty room.

* * *

He'd railed against solar, wind, and other clean, renewable energy sources. After all, this was and always would be Oil Country. Tom Prince didn't separate his politics from his religion. Turbine and solar panels were, from his lofty pulpit, as against the Good Book as butterfly sanctuaries. Hell—any wildlife sanctuaries. Everything belonged to men. Some men, anyway.

Still, it pleased him to see the network of newly installed solar collectors greedily lapping up sunlight from across the vast roof of the parking garage and three enormous wind turbines turning in the day's breeze, feeding power into the church. Into him.

His gaze again lifted. The church, with its seven stained glass panes, each a specific color, none of the windows decorated in holy likenesses only those fractals, glowed among its fortifications. How jagged the Holy Lamb of Prospero looked—like a cathedral made of thorns. All the barbed wire strung around the perimeter and the gun emplacements defending sacred ground added to the analogy.

He reached down, patted the sidearm in its holster, and then, unable to resist the temptation, grabbed his crotch. The king strutted forward into the heart of his kingdom. On the march, a realization struck him. *Starting today, my servants will be expected to bow before me.*

* * *

A DREAM WITHIN A DREAM

Her daily podcast message delivered, Marjorie Prince saw that the new god and his troops had returned, their objective secured. Energy crackled through her blood—surely enough to kill all Crimson or any other plague organism under the righteous power of the Divine.

She checked herself in the acre of mirror along one wall in her private office. The tan, tailored dress showed off her curves tastefully. The diamond earrings weren't too showy, though she wore her hair back to make sure everyone saw them. Her expensive shoes completed the ensemble. The pair had cost a small fortune, but you couldn't expect the mother of the second coming to wear department store shoes anymore than ride around on a donkey.

Composing herself, Marjorie exited her private stronghold. Most of the other rooms and offices sat empty. With the global crisis, the businesses that had paid top dollar for space had shuttered and weren't likely to reopen. Her heels unleashed an echo both ominous and majestic, she mused. With a thousand troops already stationed inside the church's property and makeshift housing thanks to trailers in the garage, the offices could be utilized in other ways besides storage.

One of the doors stood open. Marjorie's expression soured. She continued toward its threshold. Inside, Kenzie paced in front of a tall window, the baby cradled in her arms. Upon noticing Marjorie's arrival, Kenzie ceased her stride. Their conversation passed mostly through reflection.

"Your husband's back," Marjorie said, not bothering to conceal her tone.

"I know."

"Then, perhaps, you could do something to make yourself look more presentable for him."

Kenzie rolled her eyes, which showed bags from another long night. "Don't start with me, Marjorie. I'm exhausted enough without going another round with you."

Marjorie laughed, the short, sharp retort lacking all humor. "You'd never survive it, dear. Change out of those rags. Put on some makeup. Make the effort for the most powerful man in the new world and try—oh yes, try—to remember just how lucky you are."

The verbal slap delivered, Marjorie turned and backtracked to the elevator.

* * *

She made the tour, as she often did. In the vast kitchen, water tanks were filled with live lobsters, the walk-in freezers were stocked with whole herds of butchered beef—the finest cuts for church dignitaries, the scraps for their zealous army of believers. Dried and canned supplies left over from the church's past political fundraisers and VIP galas and goods raided from Prospero's super centers filled every space of shelf.

In what had been the choir rehearsal room, an armory now stood. Marjorie tipped a silent nod to the soldier guarding their impressive firepower. *God and guns,* she thought and continued on.

The worship hall was bathed in the radiance reflected through six of the seven towering panes of stained glass located far overhead.

The heart of the Holy Lamb of Prospero was laid out in half a dozen distinct groupings of stadium seating, with one of those stained glass panes directly overhead each section. The colors intentionally formed a progression, the first orange, the second yellow. After that, green, blue, amethyst, and amber followed. Red wasn't missing; that seventh pane loomed over the room at the back of the pulpit hidden by two enormous rolling doors.

The doors were cracked open allowing in the scarlet light raining down.

Marjorie started toward the room forbidden to most others but halted long enough to take in the image of the enormous pipe organ. Not for the first time, the pipes stretching high overhead reminded her of missile launchers. Yes, here in their stronghold, they were safe from all enemies—including the Crimson.

The room behind the pulpit was her son's inner sanctum. Black carpet covered the floor. An onyx clock, elegant and expensive—manufactured in Switzerland—tolled the seconds in ticks from one wall. The furniture was top of the line leather, suitable for a man's cave. Tom Prince's boasted the largest possible flat-screen on one wall beneath the red glare pouring down from the distant ceiling. Built-in cabinets contained the sound system and player, liquor, and plenty of hardcore entertainment. He was, after all, a man.

And such a man at that.

A DREAM WITHIN A DREAM

Tom stood at the center of the room, his back to the doors, frozen in a majestic pose that conjured a gasp from Marjorie's lips. Like a statue in his military uniform—no, a god!

"Mother," he said, at first not turning around to face her.

"I came to check on you," she said, aware that her tone from admonishing Kenzie was still there. "Someone had to."

"Are you pointing a finger at my wife again?"

She shrugged. At long last, he faced her, all emotion ironed off his expression, his handsome features hard. More blood stained his face. She hastened over and reached for his cheek. "Thomas!"

He pulled away. "It isn't mine."

Of course not—it was more blood spilled from the enemies of their new regime and applied like a trophy. The iron tang mixed with the scent of Tom's sweat triggered something dark and electric within her.

"And the mission?"

"A success."

"Of course." She set a hand on his arm. "Then it's time for you to wash up—remove the blood from your face."

He eyed her. "Is that an order? Wash your hands, Tommy, before supper?"

"No," she said, her voice barely louder than a whisper. "This Crimson has no power over you. But it's best that we remain cautious, vigilant."

"That's right, it doesn't," he growled.

She noticed his jaw clench and the flare of his nostrils. Maybe it was Kenzie's lack of respect—his wife, she should have been here to welcome him home from battle. Anger emanated off him, the waves tangible. Marjorie cupped his chin, and Tom leaned into her hand. His rage crackled out. Suddenly, he was ten again but in a thirty-three-year-old body, desperate for his mother's approval.

"It should have been a boy," he said into her palm. "She should have given me a son!"

"I know," Marjorie agreed.

She saw the blood on her hand—the sacrament he'd taken to insure their future and proof of his might. But in that moment, he was vulnerable, a child.

"Come," she said. He obeyed.

In the vast private bathroom off the room with the black carpet and red stained glass window facing the heavens, she ran hot water into the big soaker tub and unbuttoned his uniform shirt. Saying nothing, he worked off the rest of his clothes and slid down into the steaming water. Marjorie, too, traveled back through time in her memory to those ugly, lean years—always one frail step ahead of eviction, the cold baths when they shut off the electricity, the sad, unsatisfying meals made of scraps. None of their immigrant neighbors at the time ever suffered like that. No, not with every liberal, bleeding heart in the old government willing to line their pockets with gold, vouchers, and the sweat of hardworking American taxpayers.

She blinked, and it was now. More magnificent than she thought possible of any man, Tom relaxed in the tub, his big feet extended over the base and crossed at their hairy ankles. He reposed with his eyes aimed at the ceiling but likely seeing something other than the coffered design. She picked up the bar of soap and a washcloth, dunked them in the water, and washed his feet. Tom uncrossed his legs and permitted it.

"Very Biblical of you, Mother," he sighed.

She laughed. "It seemed appropriate. An ablution or baptism for he who will lead us out of the Crimson and into tomorrow."

A sound alerted her to another's presence. Marjorie looked over to the bathroom door. Kenzie stood there, her features further dulled by the steam. She hadn't changed or applied so much as lipstick.

Marjorie rose from her crouch at the foot of the tub and marched to the door, soap and washcloth in hand. Her scowl back, she dumped both into Kenzie's grasp. "Do your duty," she commanded.

Not waiting for a response, Marjorie marched out of the bathroom and across the black carpet, past the onyx clock. Crimson light rained down and, again, she pondered its significance. That panel of exquisite stained glass had been installed years before the first gruesome images had been transmitted from overseas of foreigners with bloodied faces as the life drained out of them and the plague spread across the globe.

A DREAM WITHIN A DREAM

This was the realm ruled over by Tom Prince, and he would prevail long after the last clusters of the virus died out. Man had been granted mastery over all of creation. One man in particular.

Mouth pursed and chin raised, Marjorie marched out of the room with the black carpets, her staccato muffled but surging back when she passed through the double doors and once more into the worship hall, where a kaleidoscope of bold colors cascaded down from the sky.

* * *

The supper spread was, as usual, glorious. Fine china on white linens boasted crab cakes alongside the finest rib eye from the turf. The salads were fresh and dressed up with croutons baked by the kitchen staff, who'd been offered shelter within the fortress under the agreement that they would perform their jobs for every day going forward. The red wine from their well-stocked cellar complimented both the entrée and dessert, a luscious berry parfait.

Marjorie stared into her glass, which was half empty.

"More, Mother?" asked Tom.

In his crisp suit with its red power tie, he looked a true leader. Before she could answer, Tom tipped a glance at one of the well-dressed servants. The man hastened over, a bottle in his white-gloved hands. He poured, and her eyes again fell into the color of the wine—so red, so relevant.

Kenzie seemed more interested in toying with her food than actually eating the feast her husband had guaranteed for all at the table. From the cut of her eye, Marjorie watched the pathetic other woman move her fork, testing this, poking that, but doing very little in the way of actually eating.

"Is there a problem, dear?" Marjorie asked.

Kenzie's fork scraped to a stop on the plate, the sound of the teeth across ceramic like nails on a chalkboard. Marjorie's favorite victim once more fell beneath an unwanted spotlight and looked up only to deflect from Tom's blue stare.

"I didn't sleep well last night. The baby ..."

Marjorie huffed out a dismissive laugh and raised her wine glass to her lips. Kenzie had been handed the keys to Heaven—good wine, great food, heat, safety, and, above all, Tom Prince for a husband, and yet she'd allowed herself to ignore every blessing over a condition entirely inside her head.

"Please," Marjorie snickered. "Not that tired excuse again. What would you know about postpartum depression?"

"Mother," Tom admonished.

Marjorie lowered her glass and answered Kenzie through the man seated at the head of the table. "Well, I still don't understand this ... fantasy of hers. You and I didn't have any of this." She waved a manicured hand around to indicate the elegance of their private dining room with its well-tailored wait staff. "We had nothing except for one another, and look at how well we've done!"

Kenzie bunched up her linen napkin and tossed it on the table en route to making a dramatic exit. A few sobs added to the performance. Marjorie sipped her wine, not commenting until Tom dismissed the waiters. In the stillness that followed, it was only the two of them.

"I know what you're going to say," Marjorie sighed. "That I'm picking on her again."

"No, I wasn't," said Tom.

"It's just that—of all the women you could have taken as your wife, why her? Why that boring, weak, disloyal ... squirrel?"

Tom chuckled. "Lately, I've wondered the same thing. She's nowhere near as formidable as you. Few women are."

This brought them eye-to-eye.

"Soon, we have to close ourselves away," he said. "Ride out the end—"

"—so there can be a beginning," she added.

"To have things our way."

"The only way."

"In our image," Tom said.

"After Crimson ... a new era."

"The world AC," he growled.

"AT," she corrected.

A DREAM WITHIN A DREAM

He reached for his glass and gripped the stem in his hand with enough force to snap it while raising the wine to his lips.

* * *

They made lists behind closed doors and completed them in Marjorie's office. One contained the divisions of all the labor required to operate what amounted to a small city-state within the indestructible fortress of the Holy Lamb of Prospero. With a strong military presence already secured, they mapped out the rest.

The cooking and wait staff, too, were in place, as were the cleaners expected to keep everything tidy. From the small crowd of former parishioners, vagrants, and desperates who routinely approached the gatekeepers for food and shelter within the church, they made their selections with digital thermometers—and guns—ready for even the smallest threat of Crimson infection.

They would require seamstresses, tailors, and dressmakers who could transform the fortune in appropriated textiles into one-of-a-kind showpieces for women like Marjorie Prince within the castle's walls. Unskilled laborers would be needed to assist with grunt work. Electricians, carpenters, and general contractors, too, should the building suffer any damage or require new structures be built. Some of the military personnel dabbled in mechanics, but they selected four more from the pool outside the gates that had worked at dealerships specializing in luxury models.

"Not him," Marjorie said, indicating one of the candidates. "He looks like an immigrant."

When the man tried to explain he'd been born in the community, the soldiers muscled him away from the front gate. After he insulted Marjorie over his shoulder in Spanish, they shot him dead.

* * *

The help would be housed in trailers and outbuildings—save those few that Tom selected for other duties. They would remain within easy access inside the protection of the main fortress.

Of that second list, the names were confined to one hundred—the wealthiest and most influential allies of the former church would become guests of the new city-state. Among them was Tim Madison, a young lawyer from the former high-powered firm that had represented their interests as well as a number of conservative objectives, most involving women's reproductive rights. He bought his way in with a case filled with gold. Jake Hawlette, their firebrand senator, did so with a similar tribute.

Gold. Gold would maintain its value in the new world destined to rise over the ashes of the old. In what had been the counting room where tithes had once been tallied—Pastor Tom Prince had balked at the pittance of ten-percent pre-Crimson from his flock and instead urged them to cough up thirty-three—gold filed the safe until no more room remained.

* * *

On that final day before the gates were secured from the inside, the windows sealed, and the Holy Lamb of Prospero walled itself off from the rest of the world, a limousine drew up to Tom Prince's seat of power.

The king of the new world order approached the tinted, bulletproof window at the rear of the vehicle. The glass rolled down. Inside sat Governor Cabot, his wife, and a pampered Yorkshire terrier dog that growled and snapped despite the broken little man's best effort to calm it.

"Governor," Tom addressed stiffly.

The man, in his tailored suit and impeccable winter coat, flashed a rare look for mercy that he hadn't shown to those on Death Row seeking pardons or any of society's unfortunates in the years leading up to this moment.

"Please," he begged. "For my wife and my driver."

Tom considered them. "You expect to appeal to my sense of pity?"

"If that works," Governor Cabot said.

"It doesn't. And I hate dogs—especially that kind."

Cabot's wife pulled the small terror off her husband's shattered and useless lap and attempted to calm it with a hug.

A DREAM WITHIN A DREAM

"Let me tell you why you should find a reason," Cabot said. "I know things about ruling—the ways to make those you rule behave. Means that would be frowned upon in polite society. As for why you should allow my wife to keep Little Yorkia, here ..."

The governor made a grab at the dog's neck and nearly choked it while removing its jeweled collar. He handed it through the open window to the king.

Tom examined the collar. The diamonds and emeralds weren't merely real but exquisite.

"And, if food runs low, you can always pop the yippy little monster in your oven."

Tom straightened and laughed.

The driver pulled Cabot's wheelchair out of the trunk. He eased the man, broken from the waist down, into the chair. The three latecomers proudly entered through the main gate. Tom pocketed the jewels and others offered in tribute—more currency for his future regime.

"Almost time," he whispered.

Then the grin dropped from his face, and that cold mask scanned his kingdom. Only one detail remained. He came out of the trance and marched in the direction of his fortress.

* * *

"No—you can't!" Kenzie sobbed. But he could. "She's your daughter!"

Tom seized Kenzie by the arm not holding the baby and marched her out of the room and to the stairs. A duo performance of shrieks from mother and child filled the staircase and then the vast cathedral whose main doors stood open.

"Don't, Tom. Don't," Kenzie begged.

Her words stung at his ear, effective only in cementing his decision. Soldiers waited at the main doors and a dozen more at the front gate should the king require assistance. Of course, he didn't. He tossed them out past the moat of barbed wire and chain-link erected around his domain and ordered the gate sealed. Their screams carried up, up becoming twice as loud—more than should have been possible. Higher, into the day's graying blueness.

The screams deafened.

Tom tracked them into the overcast. Far above their heads, what looked to be one of those enormous military transports was coming apart, on fire, and falling in pieces—a wing detached from its fuselage, the rest fragmenting before his eyes.

"It's time," he barked above the cacophony. "Seal it up!"

Locks were secured. Access in and out denied: 1,355 souls walled themselves off from a Crimson infected world, expecting to emerge as the rulers of whatever remained of the planet when the plague passed on, taking all that was of the past with it.

* * *

In what had been the Sunday school room, Tom worked with the weights. He pushed his muscles, sweated, and jogged up and down the six chambers of the worship hall before ending his circuit at the seventh, the room with the black carpet and onyx clock. The ritual completed, he cooled down by standing before the clock, which tolled time in a world where seconds, minutes, and hours held little meaning.

He imagined his mother continuing her podcasts from her office, spreading the good news that the righteous had prevailed and would. Everywhere in his kingdom, the faces of the chosen went about the business of their days—an elite minority supported by a servile majority. All those faces were white, all former nationalities eliminated. They were all New Americans now freed from any roots of origins to lands overseas that no longer mattered or even existed, if news of the Crimson was to be trusted.

He mopped his face with a towel, stepped out of his expensive sneakers, and padded into the bathroom, where two of his new consorts waited to bathe him. And more.

* * *

A DREAM WITHIN A DREAM

There were the usual skirmishes—impossible to avoid given tight quarters regardless of the kingdom's size. Mornings were welcomed with coffee, pastries, and stunning breakfasts of pancakes and roasted meats. Suppers were laid out buffet-style, and those who dined were expected to dress in their best: ties for men, pearls for women. On Sundays, in lieu of sermons, the king declared parties were to be enjoyed, which kept the oppressive and souring atmosphere beneath the stained glass panes as light as possible. Doable, at least.

Fewer fires burned across the horizon as weeks and then months passed. The world was running out of tinder, it appeared—the Crimson was running its course. Winter relaxed, and the days grew longer, warmer.

* * *

He'd noticed her from the start; pretty, shy though not weak like his former wife, Alma carried herself with great dignity. She was part of the team that ran the atelier and had become a favorite among his mother, the governor's wife, and other Prospero society women. She also offered haircuts to various of the husbands and single men like Jake Hawlette, who'd paid hundreds in the old world for the same privilege now given to him free.

"Do you know how many liberals it takes to change a light bulb?" Hawlette chuckled, seated in the barber's chair while Alma cut his hair to its usual perfection.

It was an old gag, one that had run on TV ads during Hawlette's last smear-filled senatorial campaign.

"None—because they'd rather keep you and the rest of us in the dark!" Hawlette said one fraction of a second sooner than in Tom's memory. "That, and, let's hope the Crimson wiped all of them out. Them and their pro-vaxxer ideologies!"

* * *

The usual skirmishes. People getting on one another's nerves. The governor's dog had nipped one of his neighbors living next door in the former conference center space. And Tom didn't care for the way Hawlette was always hanging around Alma.

He decided he didn't like Hawlette, whose jokes were staler than the air in some of the fortress's rooms and whose stupid smirk unleashed a building rage in the pit of the king's stomach.

* * *

A wintry mix lashed the night in one final gasp of March's fury. The guard signaled to the men stationed around the perimeter, always vigilant for intruders attempting to scale walls, that the king was making a rare pilgrimage out of his keep. The rear vestibule doors were unlocked to allow this. Dressed in his military finest, Tom Prince marched through the slush, across the parking lot, and to the first of the lookouts. The cold, raw air filled his lungs and cleansed him of the worsening foulness inside the castle.

"Majesty," the guards stationed below said and bowed.

Tom waved for the men to straighten and climbed up the ladder to the fortified nest guarding the northwest corner of the compound. The change of scenery exhilarated him almost as much as the frigid night air. The two men in the lookout tower bowed.

"Sit-rep," Tom demanded.

"All's quiet, sire," one man answered.

Tom reached out. The other guard handed him night vision binoculars. Tom raised them. True to the report, the world beyond was dark and still, the spring storm the only activity. He recalled something blathered on by the scientists that his political party had branded as enemies before the collapse—*We don't tell the Crimson when it's over. The Crimson is nature—it tells us.*

He exhaled a dismissive snort and made another pass with the binoculars. Nothing. Night played out in dull gray-green, the desolate landscape broken up by snow. On the final sweep, movement teased the periphery. Tom aimed the binoculars back and, for a second, no more, he saw the figure creeping through the darkness.

Gaunt, dressed in a black robe, hunched over—its face was that of a skeleton, terrible to behold. The thin layer of sweat Tom had earned in scaling to the lookout instantly turned clammy. A curtain of rain and snow billowed between him and the interloper, and when it passed, the figure was gone.

"There's someone out there," Tom said.

"Sire?" one of the guards questioned, and he received a punch to the shoulder from the other for his insolence.

"Station Delta to all eyes—we've sighted movement past the perimeter!" the wiser of the two men called into his radio.

The other nests reported in.

"Epsilon—clear!"

"Omicron—clear!"

Tom scanned the night, but the binoculars only showed a wasteland.

"Probably some straggler on his last leg," the first guard said. "Not a lot of them around anymore, but from time to time …"

Tom considered the explanation and decided to buy it.

Because the thing he'd seen looked like Death.

* * *

Shaken, Tom moved before the obsidian clock and listened to the cadence of seconds being measured. *A dying straggler, that was all.* Then why did the revulsion sit rancid in his gut and the chill linger atop his flesh? As the seconds drew out into minutes, perhaps longer, it struck him that he was listening to his own rapid pulse as it hammered in concert with the ticks of the clock.

He blinked, exhaled, and moved into the bathroom to splash water on his face. Steam drifted around him, gray-green like the view as seen through night vision specs. Until she spoke, he hadn't realized there was someone in the soaker tub.

"Problem?" his mother asked.

* * *

As she often did after delivering the good news of the day through her podcast, Marjorie made her tour of the castle. She glided down corridors and heard the arguments, angry voices, and physical blows through sealed doors; smelled the stink of alcohol, sex, and those who had forgone bathing, and wore a practiced smile. She entered the armory, loving that the soldier on duty bowed to her—for she was the mother of their king and lord, surveyed the food in the walk-in freezers and examined the riches stored in what was now the treasure room. From there, she made her way to the atelier at the rear of the ground floor offices, having decided it was time for the dressmaker to create something new, light, and dazzling to celebrate the arrival of spring.

Bolts of expensive fabrics filled wooden shelves from the floor to the ceiling. Marjorie tracked the sound of a single sewing machine to the workroom. Various orders and repairs hung on wooden hangers in order of priority. Alma was presently repairing a guard's uniform. The former senator hovered behind her, foisting unwanted attention as Alma worked.

Hawlette covered her eyes. "Guess who?"

"The man who's going to make me stitch my fingers together if I can't see what I'm doing," Alma answered in a diplomatic tone.

Hawlette didn't relent until Marjorie cleared her throat. He righted behind the girl, and the smirk dropped from his mouth. "Marjorie."

"Senator," she said.

Hawlette set both hands on Alma's shoulders. The sewing machine's needle stopped. "I'll see you later," he said to Alma though his eyes remained on Marjorie. Hawlette then slunk out of the atelier.

When he was gone, Marjorie faced the girl. "I was thinking something in robin's egg blue, appropriate for the change in seasons."

* * *

"Tell me about your interest in her," Marjorie said.

"Who?" Tom asked before downing the top-shelf scotch in his crystal glass.

Marjorie snickered. "You know the one I mean."

"Your favorite dressmaker?"

A DREAM WITHIN A DREAM

Marjorie picked up the bottle and poured another finger into Tom's glass. "You have a problem."

Tom laughed. "Only one?"

He moved in front of the obsidian clock, aware of his mother at the periphery while the majority of his focus remained on the hands tolling the meaningless information of time.

"Jake Hawlette is also interested in Alma. I'm not sure she's right for you, but she's definitely an upgrade from—"

"Don't say her name!"

"Very well. My point being that there's another rooster flexing his cockscomb under your roof, son. I've delivered the warning. What you do with it is up to you."

She departed. Tom studied the obsidian clock. His mind wandered back to that night and the guard tower. The visage of Death evaporated. Alma replaced it. Tom turned away from the obsidian clock.

* * *

Hawlette entered the room with the black carpet glowing with non-color beneath the red stained glass window, helped along by two of the castle's trusted guards. Tom sat in the leather club chair that was now his throne, dressed in his military uniform, one leg and its booted foot crossed over the other in a jaunty, regal pose. The former senator wore his power suit and tie, his hair in its usual impeccable condition, not one strand out of place.

"Was it necessary to have an escort?" Hawlette groused.

Tom smiled. "Wait outside," he said to the guards.

The two soldiers bowed and departed. Tom uncrossed his legs and stood. "Drink?"

"I'm good," Hawlette said. "What's this all about?"

Tom moved to the liquor cabinet but didn't open it. "You've been seeing Alma, the girl who makes dresses."

"So?"

"That will end immediately," Tom said with his back turned to his guest.

Hawlette folded his arms and assumed a defensive stance in the reflection cast by the cabinet doors. "Why?"

"Because I have commanded you to."

Hawlette's attitude remained at its entitled level. "And I'm to do that because … you tell me? You want her for yourself!" An arrogant snort of laughter followed the statement. "All those hot blondes you keep parading around and in your stable aren't enough for you, buddy?"

"Buddy?" Tom parroted in a voice not much louder than a whisper. "I'm not your buddy. I'm your—" He whirled, tossed the punch, and nailed Hawlette in his smug, dimpled cheek. The unexpected savagery knocked Hawlette backward and across the black carpet. "—God!"

Hawlette rubbed his jaw and shot a hate-filled look back at Tom, one that telegraphed what was to come. Tom understood the show of defiance, and Hawlette didn't disappoint. He scrambled up, howling, and threw himself at Tom. Behind them, the double doors rolled open, and the king's bodyguards hurried in, seizing Hawlette and pulling him off Tom.

Tom straightened. As Hawlette struggled between the soldiers, Tom caressed the other man's sweaty face, one stray lock of hair at long last dislodged out of alignment, a rivulet of blood seeping from the corner of Hawlette's mouth below where he'd been decked.

Tom drew back and wiped the other man's blood across his cheek, that familiar sign of conquest over a hated enemy. Then Tom shook his head.

"No," Hawlette spat.

As the guards shouldered him out of the room, he pleaded for forgiveness.

* * *

The gallows were constructed in the worship hall beneath the rainbow cast by the six stained glass windows. As the citizens of the Holy Lamb filed in, taking seats under the not-so-subtle threat of armed guards, the double doors to the room with the black carpets opened. Tom strutted out with Marjorie at his right. They proceeded to

A DREAM WITHIN A DREAM

the two thrones set on the proscenium behind the gallows—the best seats in the house.

Voices quieted, all save Hawlette's. The soldiers led him in naked apart from the zip-ties that bound his wrists and a purple jester's cap on his head after his precious hair has been shaved down to scalp.

"Let this be a lesson to all of you," Tom declared in a commanding voice that re-ignited the fire and brimstone tone once so common in the worship hall. "What you have here is a privilege not a right. Sinful behavior will no longer be tolerated!"

Hawlette kicked and struggled to no avail. "You are not a god! You're not even a man!"

"Do not speak his name in vain!" Marjorie called above the dying echo of Hawlette's outburst.

"He isn't God. He isn't!" Hawlette shrieked until the executioner standing in readiness to pull the lever releasing the trap door slapped a length of duct tape over the jester's mouth.

"So much for last words," Marjorie chuckled.

Horrified and unsure of what else to do, those assembled to witness the king's holy wrath laughed as well.

The guards forced Hawlette onto the stage. The executioner fixed the noose around his neck and pulled it tight. The seconds after that dragged on with maddening slowness—for none worse than the accused, who fought against his plastic shackles until the trapdoor dropped out beneath his feet, and the noose strangled the life from him. The body dangled, twitched, and then went still. The bells in the jester's cap continued their tintinnabulation for another moment and soon quieted.

An effective silence settled over the vastness until someone in the audience applauded, and the rest of the gathered followed suit.

* * *

The skirmishes ceased. Those within the fortress walls took more care with dressing and bathing. A solemn pall hung over the Holy Lamb of Prospero.

Tom walked with his hands clasped behind his back into the atelier where Alma worked on a dress in a milky shade of blue.

Upon seeing him, she stopped sewing and jumped up, her head bowed. "Sire," she said.

Tom forgave Alma her sheepishness. "Stop, I'm not here as your king."

"Pardon my bluntness, but I've twice now seen the folly of making that mistake."

Kenzie and Hawlette—the audacity that she would invoke their memories. So she had backbone after all. Tom's interest in her doubled. He crossed his arms and leaned against a rack of textiles in what might have seemed a casual pose on anyone else but on him, he assumed, was intimidating.

"Are you afraid of me?"

"Only a fool wouldn't be," she said, her eyes inching higher to greet his. "I'd say the entire community hides beneath the shadow of what you did."

"He attacked me."

"They only remember his end."

"Then we should give them something new to remember. A reason to rejoice."

He stepped closer and extended his hand. Alma hesitated. "Would you do me the honor?"

"Of what?"

"Joining me for a party to celebrate all that I have built here. A grand party. No, a ball—with music and dancing. Even better, a masquerade!"

She took his hand but never smiled.

* * *

A lightness washed over him helped along by what he sensed would be a reward at the culmination of the night. Sex was easy and plentiful for the king of the castle, but having a wife at his side to help him rule would, he believed, resolve the emptiness he'd known since his first marriage's dissolution. Alma would give him a son.

"Marriage?" Marjorie pressed. "Are you sure?"

A DREAM WITHIN A DREAM

"Very, Mother," Tom answered.

He stood before the obsidian clock, the sparest of smiles displayed. She smoothed out the shoulders of his uniform, picked off lint that wasn't there, and frowned.

"Isn't this sudden?"

He turned to face her. "Out there, beyond our kingdom, is a world to be reclaimed. I will take it for us."

"But is she worthy of you?" Marjorie cupped his cheek.

Tom turned away and strode to the liquor cabinet. "Don't you have things to do? Preparations to make for the masquerade?"

She considered him, most of her sudden anger concealed. "Why, yes, King of the World, I do." Saying nothing more, she left him, the staccato of her heels echoing and waning through the vastness of their cathedral.

* * *

Costumes were made with speed and diligence from long bolts of silk-satins—yellows and oranges, greens and blues, purples and ambers, all to mirror the colors of the stained glass above the heads of the future party guests. And one gown in fiery red at Tom's request to match that above the room with the black carpet and obsidian clock. Alma even constructed a matching red mask in stiff fabric that covered the face and hair.

"A show of solidarity against the Crimson?" she asked Tom, who eyed her with desire.

"That ... and more. You're amazing."

This conjured a smile. "Promise me you'll save me at least one dance in my red costume, Tom."

"I plan on saving all of them for you."

They kissed. She slipped on the red mask, and, for a terrible instant, he thought he must have been facing off against the devil. Tom's arousal continued in spite of his revulsion. Maybe because of it.

* * *

Preparations were finalized. The menu would include the best of what remained of the produce, caviar, and meats. Colorful bunting and streamers left over from when the church had hosted conservative political fundraisers decorated the former worship hall. A playlist Tom selected from his favorite Gospel, Country, Rap, and Rock CDs would play over the sound system. Gentlemen had wives press their trousers. Wives dressed in the kaleidoscope of gowns and costumes that matched the stained glass windows.

* * *

She glided down the corridor to the atelier located at the back of the megachurch's ground-floor offices, that practiced smile on her face. With her pulse barely operating above its normal rate, Marjorie followed the sound of the sewing machine. En route to her destination, a bold stroke of red color caught her eye. The flowy gown was draped on its hanger. The red mask gazed out from the shelf above it.

"Magnificent," she gasped.

The whirring cadence of the needle stilled. "Your son thinks so," Alma said, suddenly at Marjorie's side. "He requested that color for me and me alone."

"About that ..."

"Yes?"

Marjorie folded her arms. "You're an excellent dressmaker, dear, but this won't play out like in one of those old soap operas from a bygone era when the rich and handsome hero marries the lowly, pretty slice of ass from the bad section of town."

"Who said anything about marriage?" Alma fired back.

"Oh, *he* did. When it was just about fun, I was fine with it. My son is, after all, a man."

"I thought he was a god."

"Made manifest in the male form and, as such, prone to male needs. But marriage? No, dear. Forgive my bluntness, but you're not good enough for that. My son already wed one spineless girl far beneath him. I'm afraid you're fated to remain here, sewing buttons and patching up tears and nothing more."

"So you say."

At this, Marjorie laughed. "Perhaps you don't understand how it works. What I say is gospel."

"We'll see about that."

Alma started past her. Marjorie drew the hunting knife she'd appropriated from the armory from her pocket and drove it down to its handle through Alma's back. The girl got out something unintelligible—a dying comeback delivered through tongues as her legs failed and she dropped, her chin striking the floor with a loud and jarring crack.

* * *

She rolled the body in a shroud of upholstery fabric and dragged it out the rear vestibule after dismissing the guards and demanding the key. That part of the building was close enough to the dumping ground that she managed to do the deed on her own. A brisk, gray wind blew over the desolate patch of asphalt, but it refreshed her after so long inside the sealed fortress. The barrier of chain-link and barbed wire rose up. Marjorie worked the rear gate open and hauled the corpse the rest of the way through into No Man's Land, where eighteen other dead bodies had gone—one wearing a jester's cap, a few that had expired either by natural causes or suicide, others removed in secret and by design, and the picked-clean carcass of one small dog.

She caught the putrid charnel smell on her next breath and, turning, vomited up the remains of her breakfast. Marjorie righted. This was far enough. Even if Tom found out about her crime, he wouldn't remain mad at her for long. They had a special bond—one that was certainly stronger and ran deeper than his attraction for a working class seamstress.

She straightened and spit down at the shrouded body. The wind lifted and moaned around her in a ghost's keen. It struck her that she stood past their kingdom in what was to become the new world. Everywhere she turned, the landscape looked desolate and dead. It was spring according to the calendar, and yet nothing much green marked her surroundings. Apart from the necrotic breeze, the only sound came in a kind of slither that her mind translated into feathers rustling but doing so in secret. She tracked them into the pile of decaying remains.

One of those corpses—it moved!

Gaunt, dressed all in black, it hunched in a manner that suggested it was feeding on the dead. Marjorie gagged. The figure turned its face, and she froze at the horror of what amounted to sallow skin stretched over skull. She blinked, and the image was replaced by that of a large black bird with hungry eyes.

The raven jumped off of the human remains and right at her, its great wings spraying her face with the dusty residue of its feathers and something else, something worse. Marjorie screamed and staggered backward, tripping over the dead girl. The raven soared away, leaving her clutching at her chest. She coughed, sickened. Even then, she sensed the foulness in her lungs, inside her.

When next the wind gusted, it sounded to Marjorie's ear like laughter.

* * *

He dressed in an impressive black and white tuxedo and donned the simple red mask that hid the top of his face from above his nostrils to his forehead but not his eyes. Tom examined himself in the bathroom mirror. He approved of how regal he looked. She would, too. How could Alma not? He was the king of the new world. None—not even Crimson—was more powerful than the living god who ruled from his fortress.

He examined the ring he'd procured from the treasure room—a stunning marquee-cut ruby flanked with diamonds. It had been part of the governor's buy-in. Smiling, he pocketed it and started toward the double doors only to again freeze beside the obsidian clock. It was just shy of eight. Tom waited. The clock struck the hour, and he thawed.

"Let's rock," he called above the gongs.

A DREAM WITHIN A DREAM

* * *

Music poured forth over the sound system. Trays of canapés and crystal flutes filled with champagne made passes around the dance floor that formed in front of the stage where the king sat, taking in the festivities. Outside, the clouds broke and an obscenely full moon rose higher into the sky, its light at night striking the stained glass panes with an effulgence as bright as the noonday sun's.

A sappy country tune from the band Rusty Bumper concluded, and the women in their gowns and husbands in tuxedos stopped to applaud. The song that followed was a classic waltz. Some sat. Others continued the revelry, all those ballroom lessons in the life that was over finally put to use. A spectrum of colors swept across the dance floor mirroring each of the stained glass windows save the seventh.

Where was Alma?

The festivities continued. Dancers danced. Champagne got sipped and caviar consumed. More light spilled down through the windows, and laughter sounded, though it seemed desperate to the king.

As if, after this night it, too, would be a thing of the past.

* * *

The music waned, and silence replaced it. From the direction of the stadium seating beneath the purple windowpane, a figure dressed in red appeared. Tom rose from his throne, his focus captured by the vision. The woman in red glided down the stairs, her movements graceful, liquid. The red devil mask she wore added to her allure. Tom choked down a heavy swallow and discovered that his mouth had gone completely dry.

The revelers parted. The vision in red pirouetted, slinked closer. She made it to the base of the stage. Two men in tuxedos and masks boosted her up to him. She smelled of expensive perfume and forbidden pleasures. The red gown drifted around her like tongues of flame as she performed another spin.

"Alma," Tom growled.

He drew her toward him, knelt before her, and pulled the ring box from his pocket. Tom slid the ring with its red, red ruby onto her finger. A deafening applause sounded. In its wake, she nodded. Tom rose and crushed his mouth over hers.

"Yes," she sighed.

Tom stepped back. The rush of heat pulsing through him cooled. He backed away shaking his head. The vision glided closer. Tom whirled and staggered through the double doors into the inner sanctum carpeted in black beneath a red radiance. She pursued.

He made it through the glare raining down from the glass and over to the obsidian clock. There, Tom wiped his mouth. She reached for him. Tom tore the mask from her head and gazed down at the wearer's true identity.

At first, he laughed, the timbre of his own voice maniacal to his ear. The desire in her eyes both tortured and sickened him. One emotion waned, nearly driven out by his urge to kiss her again, claim her as his own, until he saw the fresh streak of crimson that had opened on her lips on the right side—the very lips he had blasphemed with a kiss.

Another cracked wide on her forehead. Blood wept out. A third lesion appeared on her neck. Revulsion filled him. Tom backed away. The obsidian clock gonged, striking the first of twelve notes to signal midnight had arrived.

The hour had not traveled alone. Behind the woman in red, who had only just noticed her condition and, clutching at her bloodied face, let forth with a sharp scream, a figure dressed in black appeared from the glow of sanguine moonlight. It eyed Tom with its sunken, skeleton's eyes. His next breath filled with the foul mix of perfume and a fetor of rot.

The figure turned and hurried out of the room and into the scene of the masquerade. Tom pursued. When he got to the stage, where he'd so often preached on the wages of sin, he saw it, the thing from the wintry night, moving by the governor's wheelchair and among the architects of his new world. It passed among them with ease and frightening speed. As the last strike of the hour gonged at Tom's back, someone screamed.

"The Crimson!"

OBLONG

Before the crash.

Before Tyrone Wyatt became *the Tyrone*—a single-name celebrity like Madonna or Sting or Prince, America's answer to Banksy.

Before all of that, there was the blood and what he did with it.

I told all of this to my editor—the story about Tyrone and the blood. Not long after, on a late summer morning, I parked my rental, exited into the warm drizzle, and approached the train station. The cars of the *Independent Traveler* stretched along the tracks, more than a dozen, all silver and oblong in design.

A strange emotion embraced me. Maybe it was the subject matter of the article I'd been assigned that brought me so far south to the Carolinas: Tyrone Wyatt, my old buddy from the Greater Albany Area where we grew up. I remembered the blood, how he transformed it, and a shiver crept down my backbone despite the unpleasant humidity. In this snapshot my mind took, the train waiting to whisk us north to New York City and Tyrone's new gallery show at the famed Brooklyn Museum of Art had also transformed. For a terrible moment, the train cars were all empty, oblong silver coffins stretching out and waiting to be filled.

* * *

I found the right passenger car, stored my luggage—one rolling case on wheels and my Italian leather valise containing pens, paper, tablet, and headphones—and slumped into the moderately comfortable window seat, knowing that after the first day of the long journey up the East Coast I'd be cursing it and begging for my own bed.

Exhaustion overwhelmed me—the flight south from Manhattan, the last minute details, and the scope of the next leg of the voyage all conspiring to erode me. It would have been so much easier if Tyrone had simply boarded a plane.

"He doesn't fly," his rep said in my memory, speaking the words with caustic hauteur.

I sunk down as far as the seat allowed, feeling damp and itchy all over. Of course, he didn't. One of the privileges of being Tyrone was that his previous incarnation, Tyrone Wyatt, had already paid his dues and suffered for his art. Certainly more so than I ever did, which is what made this penance long overdue.

The drizzle ramped up to rain. It spattered the window at my right. And I remembered the blood.

* * *

So we weren't the most popular kids in school and might have, in fact, been the least.

"Art fags," John Palmers used to taunt.

He was tall and popular, walked with a swagger, and loved him some him. He made bullying Tyrone and me a kind of blood sport. Oh yes, the blood.

The thing about Tyrone Wyatt was that he was constantly drawing and creating art. I mean with an obsession unlike anything I'd ever seen and have yet to a decade on from Rennsalier, New York. Every scrap of paper, each pen, pencil, marker, or stick of chalk was his to utilize. While the rest of us had our noses in books, the blackboard in Quiet Study became a grand mural with Greek columns and statues. In Biology class, he laid open his frog in chalk on the stretch behind the teacher's desk, the drawing so precise as to be lunatic. He was never without his sketchpad. Instead of math and other homework, he drew. Sculpting and 3-D arts came later. My friend was great at every medium he tried.

I'll admit to a modicum of jealousy, because while I loved to draw—buildings and vehicles mostly—I was nowhere near as good as Tyrone, who was the very

A DREAM WITHIN A DREAM

definition of Artist. Nor was I as devoted. You don't make a living at it, more than one well-meaning relative said whenever I showed them my efforts. And I listened.

But not Tyrone. There was no other life. It was all that he cared about, all that he was. And, on that ugly day in our sophomore year, he proved it. I watched him bleed for his art.

It wasn't unusual for the brooding kid whose face was always in a sketchbook to draw the unwanted attention of the knuckle draggers and ass-hats at the top of the idiotic social food chain at Rennsalier High. Once, a Cro-Magnon named Phil Smyth, thinking himself quite witty, knocked the current sketchbook out of Tyrone's hands in the hallway between periods and stomped all over it with his muddy sneakers. Tyrone was furious after recovering the defiled treasure but then methodically turned the wreckage into new art by incorporating the pattern of his enemy's treads into the sketches.

And so it was with the blood.

John Palmers, who considered himself the biggest gift to the world, cornered Tyrone in the school's library. Tyrone, lost in the throes of creativity, had missed the bus. I'd gotten caught up in homework by the time I realized I, too, would be hoofing it home. Palmers and his two dumb jock cohorts, well, they were never in any real hurry to leave the indestructible brick building because once they did, their lives had officially peaked.

That's what Tyrone shouted when they cornered him near the lockers outside Ms. Urbielonus' Earth Science classroom. She was grading papers when I hammered on the door for help. Palmers and company, hanging around after the final bell and shooting hoops or some other inane way to waste time involving balls, had decided to have a little fun with the Artist. The Artist, though outnumbered, fired back not with his fists but in verbal forecasts.

"One day, I'll be rich and famous, and this—*this* is all you miserable losers will ever know!" Tyrone spat.

It was a bold declaration and one that earned him the first of several punches. Matt Regen ripped the sketchbook out of Tyrone's grasp.

When the Artist reached for it, screaming, "Give it back!" Palmers slammed his face into the lockers.

The entire incident lasted, perhaps, two minutes; given the chaos, no more than three in my fractured memory of that time. But what I recall most is how, bleeding from his split lip and nose, with Ms. Urbielonus shrieking at the mean kids, Tyrone recovered his sketchpad and painted with his own blood, transforming it into art and him into the genius who'd one day rule the American art scene.

* * *

My editor at *Blanc Canvas* magazine wanted me to tell the definitive Tyrone Wyatt story for our readers, and the anecdote about the blood and how he transformed it sealed the assignment. I hadn't spoken to Tyrone for a decade. Few had. Up until the last instant, it didn't seem hopeful that he'd consent to my request. But the name of Byron Jalbert still held enough cred to get me aboard the *Independent Traveler* for the long journey north to New York City.

I learned that Tyrone had booked three of the private sleeping cars—one for him and his wife, another for the two trusted hired men who'd guard not only him but also his art, and a third to act as a kind of temporary studio space.

While sleep threatened to claim me, I saw the procession arrive and came out of my fog. The two men were taller and more formidable than John Palmers and his ilk, but I knew everything that had happened owed to Tyrone's need for capable protectors. They exited a dark SUV, one holding an umbrella over the head of the vision dressed in black that was, I assumed, Morella Wyatt, his wife. Then the Artist stepped out and I caught myself holding my breath at the image of him—slender, pale, his dark hair long, his clothes simple for a man who'd amassed millions through deep pocket collectors salivating to own his work and an endless factory assembly line of deals and assignments. In a basic white T-shirt, jeans, and sneakers, he could have been anyone, not the darling of the art world. As I thought this, I recalled Crumb in his peasant's attire and Warhol's ripped shoes. It wasn't about appearances to the genuine article; all was for art and its creation. My own body, at that very instant, sported hundred-dollar kicks and brand name jeans. Like I said, I hadn't suffered for my art. Nor had I lived for it.

A DREAM WITHIN A DREAM

After Mrs. Wyatt had been escorted onto the train, and while the Artist remained standing in the downpour—no doubt recording the experience for future endeavors, his two strongmen struggled an oblong wooden box from the back of the SUV and onto the train. I watched, intrigued, as they maneuvered it into the car. A simple pine box, I sensed that its contents were anything but ordinary. That trove contained whatever extra treasures were traveling north to the exhibit. A fortune in Tyrone. A mystery.

The Artist was the last to board. I stared out, my heart in a sudden gallop, for I experienced a slither of the lovely passion that was daily and commonplace to my friend from that former life. It was as if I was in the presence of greatness. As if? I *was*.

* * *

The *Independent Traveler* began its journey and picked up speed along the tracks. The storm chased us. The remains of a hurricane that had died and downgraded before reaching Cape Hatteras, it seemed in no hurry to fall apart completely and was predicted to travel with us up through the Mid-Atlantic States and along the East Coast before blowing out to sea. Rain hammered the exterior of the train and ran in rivulets along the outside of the windows.

We had days to go until we reached our destination, plenty of time for me to catch up with my old friend and interview him for the magazine. Still, I grew anxious as the train clacked over tracks, sped through tunnels, and chugged into the windy, overcast day. The image of the oblong box that had preceded Tyrone onto the *Independent Traveler* hovered out of focus in my exhausted mind, the mental image always there whether my eyes were open or closed. An hour after departure, I pulled my valise out of the storage rack and powered up my tablet. But I soon abandoned that for my notebook. I realized I hadn't packed a sketchpad or artist's pencils. More so, that I'd stopped carrying such things with me for some time. So I opened the notebook, uncapped a black roller-ball pen, and sketched a rectangle. Another followed, and a dozen more after that until I'd filled an entire page. None of them looked particularly good.

A sense of melancholy washed through me. Some of it could be blamed on fatigue, sure. Another slice of the pie chart belonged to going there—back to memories of Rennsalier High and the unpleasantness of those four years. The lion's share, however, was in the present state of my creativity. Tyrone had suffered more than I in high school and had channeled his sorrows into the perfect marriage of art and commerce. Everything was fodder for his muse, and he'd used that sturm and drang to heights only he had dreamed of and believed possible.

Me ... I had a useless art degree, wasn't making art, and reporting on other talents who did while standing outside the scene at its periphery looking in.

I stared at my lackluster geometric shapes.

"Coffins," I whispered.

Entombed within those hatch marks were all of my dreams.

* * *

The dining car served a limited number of sandwiches in boxes with drinks, potato chips, and fruit if you were lucky enough to place your order before the supply ran out. If that happened, I was told the only alternatives were power bars and jerky. I snagged an actual lunch box, thinking myself quite lucky, until the door to my car opened and a tall, imposing figure of a man strutted in. I recognized him from the train platform now hours at our six. He was one of Tyrone's strongmen.

"Byron?" he asked, his voice a deep, menacing baritone laced with a soupçon of something Eastern European.

"Da," I said, which seemed much more clever in my mind than spoken. "Or Ja." When that failed to elicit a smile, I added, "Yes, I'm Byron."

"Tyrone sent for you."

The statement both amused and offended me. The Tyrone I knew never summoned anyone. But Rennsalier High was a long time in the rearview, and the once bullied had become royalty, transforming like blood applied to blank sheet.

I grabbed my valise, slung it by the shoulder strap, and carried my lunch. I hadn't fully gotten my train legs so I wobbled after the muscular giant who'd already claimed his. We passed up through two cars and into the first of the private sleepers.

A DREAM WITHIN A DREAM

Based upon the few details I noted through the open cabin door, this was where Tyrone's bodyguards were berthed. On to the next, the middle, and my guide knocked on the closed compartment. The door slid open, and there stood my high school friend.

"Byron," he said with what looked like a practiced smile displayed on his thin lips.

Neither of us seemed to know what to do next—shake hands or embrace. Clearly, we hadn't traveled that far from our awkward pasts to be free of old roles. I initiated one—the trusty bro hug—while Tyrone the other, a loose handshake.

He'd always been slender. I remembered Tyrone's reluctance to eat in the school cafeteria in front of others, and how he'd scurry into some corner, usually alone, to draw. Time and fame hadn't added much in the way of meat to his skeleton. He was the same dark, haunted presentation only a decade older. What was different could be seen in his eyes. Those showed confidence, a level of cockiness, more so a degree of control. In his meteoric rise to success, Tyrone Wyatt had seized the one thing he'd never claimed in his teen years: popularity.

"Come in," he said, stepping aside. "You look great!"

"You, too," I said—mainly because that was expected. The truth was, he didn't, even in his humble attire. Also, as he welcomed me into those tight accommodations, an unpleasant odor stirred the normally reassuring smells of paint and thick, old school turpentine. A canvas stood on an easel, and upon it the first brushstrokes of black had been applied and glistened. The bunk remained folded up. Bracing it was the oblong pine box, partially hidden by a drop cloth. A miniature but impressive artist's studio had cropped up in the middle of Tyrone's three private cars.

He extended his hand toward the pine box, inviting me to sit. I did and again wondered what exquisite artworks rested beneath my weight and the box's lid. I looked at my lunch, no longer hungry despite the hole in my stomach.

"You can dine with Ella and me tonight," Tyrone said. "We've made arrangements—much better than what they're passing off to everyone else in that dining car."

"Very generous," I said.

I watched him as he lifted his brush and palette, took to the spot before the canvas as the train raced ever forward, and the bitter smell in the room crept closer, closer.

"It's great to see you again after all this time," I said.

Tyrone eyed me from the periphery and painted. "I agree. Back then—in the insanity of that low place where we were forced to mingle among the lowest, I enjoyed our many conversations on the artist's life."

I smiled at the memory. There had been quite a few of those sessions. I remember the afternoon at Tyrone's father's house getting lost in talk of what we would do, where we'd go, once we graduated high school.

"New York," I said. "Center of the American art scene."

To this, he'd dismissed my answer with a laugh. "New York? Filled with critics and pretentious wannabes? Not to mention the cold winters. No, I'm going someplace where it's warm."

His father, who'd paid zero attention to Tyrone, kept the heat on a paltry sixty-two degrees in January. Was it any wonder, given the gulag living conditions, why he always looked so thin, his complexion like that of a mushroom?

"You did it," I said. "Look at you. Hell, you must have broken some rule to be able to sneak turpentine onto a passenger train."

This brought a tight little smirk in response. "You could say I've done well."

Now, back in the present, it was my turn to snort.

"And you? You work for the magazine," he said, which sounded so polite in its delivery I wondered if I was really hearing Tyrone's disappointment.

"Yes," I said.

Contemplative silence followed. The Artist painted. The train pounded over the tracks. The dying hurricane pursued.

"It takes a lot to keep going day after day after day," he said in a voice not much louder than a whisper, the volume turned so low that, at first, I couldn't be sure if it was real or I'd imagined the words. "The kind of passion to produce and keep producing, to mine what little is left inside you for inspiration after you've already hollowed out your imagination like a Halloween jack-o'-lantern scooped of pulp and seeds down to the shell."

A DREAM WITHIN A DREAM

I settled back as much as the angle of the oblong box and raised bunk allowed. "So you're like the sun burning up its hydrogen on its way to going supernova?"

Again, that laugh and spare grin. "Well put. What I meant was ... not everyone's cut out to be a serious artist."

"What makes one artist more serious than another?" I challenged.

This earned me a look through Tyrone's narrowed eyes. "One talks about art, dabbles, dances around in a disguise, but never gets close enough to the hydrogen to feel its full heat, only its warmth from a distance. The other lives, eats, breathes, sleeps, and dies by the fire of his passion. He feasts upon the hydrogen while it's lit up and white-hot, not caring if he gets consumed in its righteous flames. Shall I tell you about my first years in what we'd call 'the art business?'"

I reached for my valise, resting at my right leg. "Should I be taking notes or recording this?"

"No, this is a reunion between friends not the interview. That can come later, Byron. Think of this as you and I catching up. Okay, so after graduation, I packed up my sketchpads and supplies and two garbage bags full of clothes into my rusty, used car and I drove, just drove, south—to get as far away from my father and that house as possible. Ran out of gas twice. Sketched while I waited for someone to help me out—the second time took a day and a half. I slept for a month in that car before taking a rented room in a house owned by a woman who was quite mad. I'm no licensed therapist, but you wouldn't need a degree to figure it out. 2 + 2 = 4 and all that. She stole from me. She treated me like a possession, not a tenant. I'm absolutely convinced that if I'd stayed there, she would have locked me in a cellar room or murdered me when I finally dropped off from staying awake. At the end, I never did sleep, no. I barely got out of there with my belongings by crawling through a window and down to the backyard, where I'm sure various other bodies are buried."

"That sounds terrible!"

"Oh yes, and it was only the start. I got robbed. My car was stolen with everything I owned inside, including my artwork. Those were later recovered in a dumpster—the thief clearly wasn't smart enough to hold onto what would now be worth millions! Twice I got evicted from lousy apartments that even the mice were ashamed to call their own. I went hungry, but by then I was a pro at that particular skill set. But you know what I did? What I constantly did to keep going, to stay white-hot?"

"Art," I said.

At this, Tyrone's smile widened, and I sensed the gesture wasn't for my benefit but his own. His brush glided across the canvas with an elegance and fragility that was beyond preternatural. If I stared too long, I sensed his moves would hypnotize me.

"I set up outside—sketches while you wait. I'd draw portraits for ten bucks in ten minutes. There was always a line. One afternoon, the Fates blessed me. The society woman who asked me to draw her was married to one of the wealthiest gentlemen in town. She was so impressed with the results that she commissioned me for a proper sitting. She told her friends. One owned a gallery in Raleigh. After that, I couldn't keep up with requests and offers. You're aware of the rest."

"Stardom, wealth, success," I said.

His focus again captured me. I wanted to shrink from Tyrone's gaze. Or run.

"See, that's my point. I never cared about success or wealth, only creating my art. As for success, my dear Byron, I felt like I'd attained that when John Palmers drove my face into the lockers, and I painted with my own blood. Because at that moment I had fully suffered for my art and knew that art would reward me."

He straightened and lowered his brush. "What do you think?"

I'd been so trained on his words and the deftness of his brushstrokes that, until that moment, I'd failed to see what he'd painted. On the canvas in bold, black strokes was a man who felt and looked older than his years seated in defeat upon an oblong box. The artistry was exquisite, the delivery as grotesque as it was honest. Captured in paint was one of those counterfeit artists he'd spoken of—the ones who dressed the part and offered lip service but masquerade on the edges of sacrifice rather than enter the flames, too afraid they'll be consumed.

He had painted me.

"It's yours, a gift from Tyrone," he said, speaking in Third Person.

Heat baked on my tongue. I nearly choked on the dryness. "Me? No, you're … that's too generous."

A DREAM WITHIN A DREAM

"Nonsense. From one artist to another."

And there was the subtle dig, because we weren't equals, never had been, and only one of us had earned the right to use that particular sobriquet.

"Consider it like the mythical money tree some people dream of finding in their backyards. You know, you need quick cash, you just wander past the patio and pick a few leaves. At today's going rate, if you sold this, you could likely retire and live a very happy life."

He leaned closer and signed it with his brush and added the trademark Tyrone teardrop, which I knew meant so much more. It was his blood symbolized in black paint.

Tyrone was right—his offer of art was like an instant windfall had been handed to me. But at that instant, staring at the honest, hideous representation of my true self, I didn't want it. I hated his gift and its giver.

"Meet us in the dining car at six," Tyrone said. "For a celebration dinner."

I nodded and stood, more than eager to escape the Artist's studio. As I rose, my movement stirred that noxious smell of turpentine and something else into the air, and I realized the latter originated from inside the oblong box.

* * *

The train charged forward.

I sank into my seat as a world half submerged in fog and rain sped past at the periphery and saw my future self in my tiny apartment alone apart from the painting. As the oil dried, it would taunt me in silence: *Portrait of a Wannabe*. A reminder that, unlike Tyrone, I hadn't given my all to that which I professed to love. I already hated the thing—hated its genius, its honesty, its ugly beauty. After weeks or months with it, I saw myself jumping out a window from the tallest building possible in order to escape. It wasn't only a painting, it was also a mirror.

Or I could sell the damn thing through one of your finer auction houses and retire before thirty. Maybe then, given the freedom, I'd go someplace remote—a cabin in the woods in the Adirondacks, Poconos, or New England, invest in art supplies and a decent amount of dark roast coffee and top-shelf liquor, try my hand, at long last, on the life of the artist I'd envisioned yet had never experienced. Only that outcome, too, was doomed to end in my blowing my brains out deep in the wilderness because, unlike Tyrone Wyatt, it was never really about the art for me.

Never really enough, anyway.

I gazed out the window and buried my focus in the indistinct vista racing past, there one instant and gone the next. A town I'd never visited and never would vanished in a blur of lights shining from the wood and brick houses, proof of lives being lived not far from the tracks. The artist in me, what remained of him, wondered about the people dining or sobbing or making love in those rooms and, to my surprise, inspiration blossomed in my gut. That strange electricity urged me to reach for my notebook and pen. But before I uncapped the pen, the car door released and one of Tyrone's two giants strode in, his face humorless.

"Dinner," he said, nothing more.

Half of me wanted to remain where I was and subsist on packaged snacks. But I remembered that I was on assignment for a feature on Tyrone Wyatt, and also that the Artist was still my friend. I packed up notebook and pen, picked up my valise, and maneuvered down the center aisle to the door. Tyrone's muscle was already gone and halfway through the next car in line.

One section of the dining car had been reserved only for Tyrone and company. The other of the giants sat in a menacing pose marking the line in the sand that none save I were permitted to cross. Already seated at the table was Mrs. Wyatt, dressed all in black, a bold stripe of electric green cutting through her dark hair. She worked on her nails, which were the same color as the highlight. The caustic stink of nail polish remover assailed my nostrils as I approached. Absent was her husband.

Morella Wyatt glanced up and smiled. "Byron? It's about time."

"For what?" I asked.

"For you to join me. I'm starving and bored. Come—sit!"

I moved past the gatekeeper, imagining him as a large guard dog with mean eyes and salivating jaws. He smelled of cologne, the kind splashed on to disguise the fact that the wearer hadn't showered. I set down my valise and slid onto the metal bench bolted to the wall—not much more comfortable than the seat I'd sleep on later in the night now that I'd grown intimate with it. As I joined her, I noted Morella's scent—far more pleasant than the guard dog's. An awkward silence fell over us, one broken only by the clack of the train's forward charge. Throughout, she eyed me. Her smile persisted.

"So ..." I said.

"Yes?"

"Where's your husband?"

She snorted a laugh—not very elegant a sound but charming. "Him? He never dines in public. It's just you and I."

I remembered high school and how Tyrone would slink off to private corners to draw, usually until some jerk like Phil Smyth or John Palmers targeted him with a projectile from their lunch tray.

"Never?" I asked.

"Not when he can be in his studio creating art," she said. "And the world is Tyrone's studio."

"Mrs. Wyatt—"

"Ella," she stressed.

"Maybe I should go until Tyrone can join us."

"Don't you dare leave me alone!"

I tipped a glance over at the guard dogs. The second had joined the first. Both were turned away from us, eyes aimed at their surroundings, brains somewhere else far, far away.

"Them?" she snorted again. "Arkadino and Ugo aren't exactly my idea of company. Lousy conversationalists."

Neither responded to her little digs. They fiddled with their phones, oblivious to what we said.

"Yeah, I see what you mean."

"This gives us a chance to get to know one another. You hungry?"

As soon as she asked, I was.

"Good. We instructed them to feed us decently during the trip, and if they don't Tyron's threatened to paint them!"

She said this with a mix of glee and mischievousness. After having been painted by her husband, I appreciated the threat and sympathized with the train's chef.

"Something to drink?" she asked.

"Sure."

Ella called for Ugo, who didn't look up. When that failed to gain his attention, she nudged his butt with her foot. Ugo jumped and turned. Ella snapped her fingers.

"Right away, Miss," the guard dog said.

Not long after, a bottle of red wine and actual glasses appeared on the table. She poured. The wine was potent—more so on my tortured, empty stomach. But I drank it even knowing the tannins would inspire a beaut of a headache.

Linen napkins and glass plates festooned with beautiful salads and rustic, garlic-forward croutons followed. A basket filled with warm herb rolls and butter. Two plates covered in cloches—underneath was the perfect salmon crusted in crushed sesame and with crispy skin served over lentils. For dessert, we enjoyed raspberry tarts and the last of the bottle's contents.

"How did you meet?" she asked, the glass held in her slender fingers.

"Tyrone and I? He didn't tell you?"

She flashed a coy smile. "He never talks about the old life. B.S."

"Bull—?"

"Before Stardom."

I chuckled, glanced away, and stared into the night beyond the dining car's windows. "We were the unpopular kids in school, so, you know, safety in numbers. We both loved to create art—him more than I."

"Naturally," she said.

Other diners who'd choked down chicken nuggets and hot dogs along with small, outlandishly expensive bags of snacks had watched us dine, their jealousy tangible. I hadn't minded that. Now, talking about my past felt like an embarrassment, the subject matter not meant for others to know.

So I deflected it back.

"How did you meet?"

A DREAM WITHIN A DREAM

"Oh, I totally wanted him for his money," Ella said with the same ease and frankness other people used to discuss the weather. "I met him at one of his first big gallery openings and told him as much. That's what he liked about me—my directness. Told it like it was. That made it easier for him to go about his work without worrying I'd betray him. Cards on the table, right up front."

I glanced back. She was charming, pretty, brash—an open book. I saw in her what Tyrone did and envied him more.

"We just sort of ... work," she said.

"And you don't get jealous?" I asked the open book.

Her expression flushed the slightest. "You mean of his mistress, his other love, the art?" I nodded. "I made peace with her a long time ago, knowing that if it came down to it, he'd choose his art over me. I'm okay with being second-best."

Despite her answer, I sensed she wasn't, not entirely. But that she'd resigned herself to the reality of their relationship.

"He has her, and I'm permitted the occasional distraction."

Again, Ella extended her leg. This time, her foot brushed against my shin. I tensed. A chill scurried down my spine cold only to surge back up hot and unpleasant. There was no mistaking what she implied. Mrs. Morella Wyatt was not the type prone to games.

"I'm flattered," I said, nearly choking on the sudden dryness in my mouth.

"You should be."

I again grew aware of the two guard dogs and the other diners beyond the moat of their protection. "Thanks for a wonderful meal," I said.

Picking up my valise, I stood and fled the dining car. At the door, I turned back to see her smiling, the discussion of distractions far from over in the Artist's wife's estimation. I pushed the release. The door opened. I continued on to my seat but didn't sleep.

* * *

Rain cascaded, and the wind of the dying hurricane screamed in a banshee's voice around the train as we barreled through the night. Where were we now—Virginia? In my crushing exhaustion, I couldn't tell. Maybe we'd traveled all the way back to Rennsalier. I'd wake to find myself inside that hated brick prison where I would be forced to scurry from classroom to classroom and hope to avoid notice by the little tin gods who'd staked out various temporary denominations within their Church of High School.

An ugly truth crossed my tired mind while I was trapped in that foggy state: how grateful I was to have been friends with Tyrone Wyatt. Not because of the art—no, that was a ruse on my part, something to bond us together. The reality was, Tyrone had spared me the brunt of unwanted attention by being a much easier and tempting target for the self-appointed and anointed false gods of Rennsalier High.

Tyrone had taken plenty of beatings that should have been mine.

I wanted to feel guilty but couldn't. High school was a decade in the rearview, and I'd let most of my rage go. Not Tyrone, apparently. It was clear in his eyes, there in his work—*Matón*, the name of his new exhibit in Brooklyn. *El matón* in Spanish translated as bully, thug, roughneck, hoodlum, bruiser. All of the works were inspired by his old enemies, who he'd vilified and immortalized in his art. By all early predictions, the show would be his most successful and best yet—and one guaranteed to line the Tyrone Wyatt coffers in fresh millions.

While I struggled to sleep, too itchy and sweaty to give up on thoughts of what I'd walked away from, I saw where Tyrone was: his makeshift artist's studio in the middle of the three train cars he'd reserved. He was in there doing what he loved and was compelled to, not caring nearly so much about anything else.

Matón.

Art had blessed him. It had also cursed him, because the scars from which it had sprung ran so deep that their wounds would never fully heal.

* * *

I washed my face and slapped on fresh deodorant. The bathroom reeked from those who'd previously used it, and the floor was damp and gritty due to men who'd missed what should have been an easy stainless steel bull's eye. But I cut the offenders some slack, because the wind chasing us from the dying hurricane creeping up the East Coast had ramped its ferocity, and the train shook worse on this morning.

My gut ached, the nausea born of a lack of quality sleep and too much wine. I needed coffee—and about a week in bed. New York was still a long way off. I wondered if, given so many stops along the way, we'd even reached the Pennsylvania border. Maybe we were still trapped in North Carolina and going in circles like Ouroboros, the mythological serpent that devoured its own tail.

I brushed my teeth again. Was washing up in a foul environment like a bathroom on a train considered suffering for one's art? It seemed so to me.

I hadn't returned fully to my seat when the door from the car ahead of mine opened and Arkadino strutted in. He waved for me, said nothing.

"Good morning to you, too," I said.

I stowed my toiletries bag and towel, picked up my valise, and followed him to the Artist's studio, where Tyrone waited to give the interview.

* * *

Photography would be handled by Dumont at the actual exhibit. Tyrone had promised to furnish snapshots from his past—including one or more from his teen years. Even so, the temptation to take some from his temporary center of operations aboard the *Independent Traveler* possessed me. When I entered, he barely looked over or acknowledged me. The intensity woven into his expression stole my breath. I wanted to be Tyrone as much as I wanted to bed his wife. The fire burned in his gaze and just beneath his skin, white-hot but not consuming him. No, it fueled him.

I was so hypnotized by him that, at first, I failed to notice what he painted. The subject was a man clad in a kind of military uniform bedazzled with medals. The epaulettes on both shoulders, upon closer examination, were made of paintbrushes, the medals the twin masks of Comedy and Tragedy, a tiny painter's palette, and other tools of the artist's trade. At the very base of the portrait, the paint all bled into a crimson puddle that appeared to suggest an ever increasing depth, eventually enough to drown the petty dictator. As for the subject himself ...

The man was almost recognizable, with a face that might have been familiar if not for its elongated forehead and hair poofed out into asymmetry. The overall presentation was unflattering, much like my portrait, as well as brutally honest.

Tyrone tipped a look at me. "Know who he is?"

"Almost," I said.

Tyrone smirked. "Oh, I'm sure you've met His Self-Appointed Lordship, gallerist and critic Jerry Powers."

There it was, so clear now that I wondered how I could have missed it. Another lapse to be blamed away on exhaustion, Powers had, early on, berated Tyrone's work and had since grudgingly admitted the error of his ways. Not that Tyrone would ever forgive him.

"You listen to these pretentious nobodies blathering on and on, not one of them knowing anything. So high and mighty in their judgment of others, and yet they've created nothing, only judged," he growled. "The modern bullies of my life. They just have better teeth and nicer shoes than John Palmers."

I removed my tablet and clicked on the record button.

"You've proven all of your enemies wrong and doled out eternal punishment upon them," I said.

Tyrone snorted. "Did I tell you about Palmers?"

I shrugged.

"I saw him not long ago."

Electricity sparked in my tortured gut. I moved over to the oblong box and sat again, aware of the foul smell it exuded, something the old school turpentine could not completely mask.

"You saw John Palmers—for real? In real-time?"

"Phil Smyth is dead, you know. Car crash five years ago. Drove his SUV drunk into an oak tree. There's a canvas in the show, one of a big, brooding oak with lots of branches and a scar carved into its trunk. If you look at the knots and scar, they look like Smyth's ugly face."

"About Palmers?"

"He showed up at my studio, threatened to sue me if I didn't pay him for the right to use his likeness in the series of portraits I was working on for the exhibit. I told him, sure, I'd toss him a few singles because that's all his face was worth. Then I'd counter sue for a few million over the abuse he put me through, which was well documented and mine to utilize as therapy in my art. But the funny thing ..."

I wondered what could be considered funny in any confrontation between Palmers and the Artist.

"So damn funny ... how small he was. I mean, I was sure his curls brushed the ceiling in high school. But here he was, shorter than me. And ten years off the baseball team and hoops court, he'd developed a hell of a paunch. Classic beer gut. Man, how my telling him these truths wounded him worse than any beating he ever delivered to me. I faced him, my enemy. He was a broken, pathetic little man, a dethroned high school god, and I was successful, rich, but, above all, still creating my art. My art was my weapon, and he was nothing."

"Amen," I said.

To this, Tyrone smiled and laughed. "Yes, so be it. Now ask your questions."

"You told me about fires, supernovas."

His grin flattened. "The spark of splitting atoms. It's the eight-pointed star of inspiration that ignited within me as a teen when I first knew art had chosen me."

"You mean that you chose art."

At this, Tyrone shook his head. "No, I had no other choice. And once I surrendered to its jealous love, I understood that if I didn't give it my all, I would burn up and vanish."

"You've given it all that you are."

"And more."

I shifted atop the oblong box while, with his façade restored, Tyrone painted.

"And this?"

At that moment the train lurched violently to one side, and we heard the shriek of the dying hurricane's breath through the clatter of tracks being crossed. We must have hit some vicious crosswinds over a trestle bridge. Tyrone swore and resumed painting.

"This?" Tyrone barely moved his head in a point toward my seat. "You mean the box?"

"Yes."

"It contains one more piece for my gallery show. A work of sculpture. The most important of all, I'd venture to say."

I confessed I thought it something valuable smuggled aboard like an original da Vinci—perhaps a found earlier version of *The Last Supper*, or one of Van Gough's works. The tragic Dutch master was, I recalled, Tyrone's favorite.

"Another original Tyrone," he said, grim-faced and back to speaking in Third Person. "Perhaps the most original of all his work."

The train lurched again. I imagined diners several cars away from where we spoke spilling their morning coffee and those in the restrooms panicking with their pants down. After that jolt, the train seemed to level out without much more in the way of wind shear.

"Tell me something about yourself, Tyrone," I said. "A secret."

Without hesitation, he answered, "I'm not a good person, but I am a great artist. I say this with no arrogance and the greatest degree of humility. I say this after having lovingly, completely given breath, body, soul, and blood to art."

* * *

Tyrone's words chased me in my sleep, mimicking the wind that buffeted the train constantly. I sensed what must have been his moment of ultimate triumph when he looked down on his former tormenter and they both knew the victim had been, at long last, proven victorious. I imagined the Brooklyn Museum of Art filled with corpses and likenesses of all who'd dared to oppose the Artist's fire and would be put on display like the trophies of a merciless hunter. Then I saw myself, stretched out on the canvas he'd painted of me—a shadow of an artist. All those oblong figures I'd sketched, none particularly good. All were coffins of my making, for I realized I would never be anywhere near as legit as Tyrone Wyatt no matter how much of myself I vowed to give to art.

I stirred, suddenly aware of a presence beside me in the dark. For a glorious moment, I hoped it was one of the Helicon Nine—a muse sent to implore me to create. Then I caught the dark presence's bitter smell of nail polish and floral perfume. Ella.

A DREAM WITHIN A DREAM

"Byron," she whispered, her voice sweeter and more bewitching than any siren's.

I turned my head and met her lips. She cupped my cheek and dug in her nails just enough to remind me of their sharpness though not to mark my face. Our kisses hungry, our tongues sought one another, and again, I hated Tyrone Wyatt for all he claimed as his and which he'd earned and all I didn't have.

The train pounded along the tracks, through the storm, and the wind shrieked around us. While we made something like love in the spare privacy offered by the night, my mind drifted beyond us, into the car where the Artist had created a studio and where I knew he was deeply and passionately at work.

* * *

At one point in the darkness, the train jolted and I came out of my exhausted state and opened my eyes. Rain still streaked the windows. Beyond, shadow-cloaked countryside blurry from the storm raced past. I guessed we were cutting across Pennsylvania.

I turned over, expecting Ella to be there, but the next seat was empty. In something of a daze, I crossed into the next car. I didn't know if I was looking for her or just walking off my guilt. The train lurched as wind slammed into it, and I nearly toppled. Somehow, I remained upright. Not far ahead, I made out the heavy screech of a hammer's claw pulling at nail heads. I tracked it to the makeshift studio's door. *The oblong box—it could only be that.*

I didn't announce myself or bother knocking. I opened the door and entered. The place reeked of turpentine and the foulness from inside the box, whose lid Tyrone had removed. He didn't notice my intrusion until the train lurched again, forcing me to brace against the wall. The violence of this latest tremor sent his easel toppling and spilled the cup of brushes soaking in paint thinner.

Tyrone looked up, and his eyes burned with fiery madness. He reached for the oblong box's lid, meaning to close it, but I intercepted him before he could and gazed down at what the crate contained.

I stole a glance in and couldn't tell what I was seeing because the level of wrongness rewrote the definition along with warping time and space. Inside was supposed to be a statue—something the Artist had created. And that was, I believe, the case. Tyrone had created the ugly work of art within the protection of the oblong box. But it had also, in reverse, created him and, like the blood on that long ago afternoon, he'd transformed it from what it was into something more.

And what it had been was John Palmers.

"My greatest work of art," he announced.

Palmers' cheeks had been painted to resemble a clown's. The horror of his death was still clear in his eyes. The body had been preserved but exuded that stench of rot I'd noticed from the moment I first entered the studio, which the turpentine could not fully mask.

In the lunatic moment that followed, it struck me that, though hideous, the work was also beautiful—Tyrone's finest!

"Magnificent," I gasped in the breathless second of a holy moment.

Everything around us silenced—the wind, the train, our voices. All I heard was a heartbeat, though I couldn't tell if it was his or mine.

And then the train jumped the tracks.

* * *

I didn't know this at the time, but in one final show of its former rage, the hurricane had picked up some momentum merging with a warm front in Pennsylvania. Enough to unleash a row of violent microbursts—localized downdraft tornados much smaller in scope but no less powerful in terms of ferocity.

The heartbeat ... an explosion in the downdraft's wake. I struck the wall. The lights crackled out. My ears rang with the screams of metal grinding against metal and passengers being tossed about. A putrid smell filled my next breath—it could have been the turpentine spilled in the crash, diesel fuel, or John Palmers' corpse reimagined as art.

The darkness bloomed with an effulgence of light. What I mistook for the power coming on was a spark from some severed outlet along with the turpentine, now ignited. The flames spread toward where the accelerant was doused—the oblong box containing Tyrone's masterpiece.

The Artist saw where the flames where headed. "No!"

I moved to stand but slipped on the uneven floor. With screams and alarm bells now filling the air along with the howl of the wind, I remembered Ella—foolish, I know, but my imperative was to reach her. I made it back to my feet, aware of the heat from the new inferno.

"Tyrone, come on," I shouted above the din.

He looked at me, his eyes glowing red in the glare cast by the fire consuming his greatest work. "Not without my art!" he spat.

I stared to speak—was that sculpture worth dying for? But I already knew the answer, and smoke filled my mouth. Then, having reached the broken door to the studio, I gazed back in time to see the flames jump from the oblong box and what it contained onto Tyrone. The tongues licked at his clothes, which must have also been soaked in turpentine, and instantly engulfed him.

He was Prometheus in that instant, Icarus. More than that, he was a supernova blazing brightly beside the oblong box before adding his unholy scream to the sudden cacophony around us.

THE CONQUERING WORM

Early on that dark June morning, a lone figure clad in a wide-brimmed hat, white shirt, and black trousers approached the grave. No onlookers waited to snap photographs or apprehend the man. The city of Baltimore mostly slumbered. The remains of a moon past full gazed down like a lone, narrowed eye.

The man carried a tote—one of those canvas shopping bags, a modern bit of stage prop in a setting from another time. Aware of the ache in his bones and, worse, his gut, he knelt before the cenotaph, which bore the image of a raven, and opened the tote. It contained a bottle of cognac, a single glass, and three blood-red roses. The flowers exuded a sweet and exotic perfume.

"I'm six months late," the man apologized while opening the bottle.

He poured, just enough for the toast, and arranged the three roses at the base of the headstone. Then he raised the glass. "To new traditions as well as old."

He drank. The cognac didn't go down smoothly, and he heard his former doctor, now three states away, reminding him not to mix alcohol with the new pills he was on. Oh well, this one infraction wouldn't kill him. And if it did ...

The original Toaster who'd visited the grave from 1930 until 2010 had likely been two; father and son it was believed. That third rose now made a kind of mathematical sense. As for the drink killing him—

Darius stood and raised his glass again. "And now, that final curtain call," he said with theatrical flourish. "The one when Death applauds us all!"

* * *

He parked behind the building and wandered out to the front. The sun had crept up from hiding, and the day's promised warmth triggered a host of summer smells—the green of the season, the nearby river, and bread baking at the closest street corner where the bushes outside the restaurant were less of a tangled mess.

Darius glanced up at the timeworn marquee. The Destination Theater had sat vacant and silent for eight years—one longer than was considered lucky and three more than it took for every cell in his body save the matter of his brain to die and be replaced, leaving him a completely different person in strictly physical terms not to mention a man burdened with cells he didn't want; ones that were, even as he stood there staring up at the building's faded royal purple and slate façade, devouring his insides.

"*Destiny*," he sighed. "I like that name better."

The Destiny Theater. *Yeah.*

He continued up the paved wheelchair access ramp, pulled a key from his pocket, and unlocked the front door. The alarm was a basic do-it-yourself bit added by the previous owner, who'd still charged top dollar for the place despite its state of abandonment.

"The last play put on here was some loony improv by a couple of college no-talents," the man said in Darius' memory from when they'd passed papers. "No wonder the place closed up after that, deader than Count Dracula." He'd then gone on to snicker at how he'd gotten the Destination Theater at cheap money through foreclosure.

It hadn't been quite so cheap for Darius.

"What do you want this musty old shoebox for?"

"The play's the thing," Darius had answered, his best theatrical smile on display—more for his benefit than the man seated across the table.

Leaving the memory behind, Darius breathed in the lobby's aged smell. The tired blue carpet exuded a staleness he worried couldn't be removed by steam cleaning alone. The tall windows showed plenty of dust made more obvious by the grimy remains of yellowed tape. Lots of elbow grease would be demanded before anyone took to the Destiny's stage.

But oh, that stage!

A DREAM WITHIN A DREAM

He removed his hat and pushed through the rightmost of the carved rosewood double doors and into the cavernous darkness beyond. Locating the light switch, Darius flipped on the elegant candelabra suspended from the ceiling. Several of the bulbs were out and needed to be replaced. Enough still burned to cast their radiance down upon the ancient seats upholstered in royal purple velvet, the walls and their exquisite wedding cake molding, and the small stage whose ancient boards showed off the scrapes of all who'd once performed there.

As had become another new tradition, Darius knelt beside the back row of seats the same way he'd done in his Catholic youth before taking to the miserable wooden pews at Saint Matthew's Church in a town far away, one he doubted he'd ever visit again. The seats at the Destination—no, the *Destiny*, his inner critic reminded—weren't much more comfortable. But they would suffice for a pair of acts and an intermission.

Again, his body reminded him of its exhaustion and worsening frailty. He straightened, descended the subtle incline to the stage, and followed the five stairs up, aware of the smell of abandonment there as well as the tingle of a shiver born of excitement teasing the fine hairs at the nape of his neck. His next breath came with difficulty. The tests for mold had come back negative—thankfully.

No, this malaise originated from within. The worm turning and chewing through healthy tissue and leaving the equivalent of rotten fruit in its wake. In his mind's eye, he saw it, fat and writhing, its teeth sharp, its lips red. Not for the first time, he wanted to cry but held in the tears. Death didn't care if you were a genius like Einstein or as talented as Van Gough. To cancer, all were the same. Just meat.

Genius or jester, cancer also didn't care if you were a former corporate cog who'd loved the theater in his youth and had always dreamed of being an actor—it had taken one of those damning come-to-Jesus, life-altering moments to force the dream into reality. Only now, it was almost too late.

Darius gazed out at the audience.

No one was there.

* * *

The task of raising the Destiny Theater from the dead was vast in scope and, on that June day, once more overwhelmed him. Nauseous, Darius crawled atop the single mattress in his private apartment at the back of the cramped office and immediately passed out.

The room boasted two windows—the first a transom over the door, the second a view down onto the rear of the building where his car was parked. Opening that window had been nearly impossible and had exhausted Darius. But he was grateful for the fresh air it allowed into the place.

As he slept, the threadbare curtains lifted in a humid breeze. Thunder rumbled in the distance. The new day darkened. Darius woke three hours later to the splashing of the rain as it spattered inside beyond the sill and ran down the wall.

Through slitted eyes, Darius watched the cascade, aware that he should move to act but too nauseous to stir. Death didn't care if you were a genius or a genius only in your heart. This thought eventually propelled him up from his stupor. In addition to a near-constant twisted stomach, he suffered from a curious condition of feeling overheated and glacial at the same time. Sweat lay clammy atop his flesh. But on his way to the window, his teeth chattered.

He pulled down on the window. Closing it against the warm rain demanded everything he had at that moment. The breeze shrieked in protest. Part of the curtain snagged in the seal. A puddle had formed on the floor.

Darius pulled a clean towel from the small stack in the apartment's tiny bathroom and draped it over the sill. A chill was all over him now. He hastened into the bathroom one step ahead of his vomit. While on his knees shivering beside the toilet, a memory from childhood rose fresh in his thoughts: the house where he'd grown up, the year when he was seven, first grade—his parents woke him for school before the sun rose. It was winter, and he was cold, so cold. In the vision, he saw his younger self waiting for them to drive him to the bus stop, huddled in a version of a fetal curl atop the furnace grate, soaking up the heat.

With the expelling of his empty guts, the temperature balanced out. His teeth stilled their chatter. But the respite was doomed to be brief, because something even more unsettling replaced that particular misery.

A DREAM WITHIN A DREAM

He heard it from someplace beyond the small apartment whose door was closed. Then he remembered the transom which opened on the darkness of the abandonment beyond. The scrape and slither sounded again, and the ice returned to embrace him. Out there, a dusty dragging along the scuffed wood floors neared. Whatever it was had made it to directly outside the door.

Had he locked the ancient metal knob with the elegant filigree design? For a terrible second, Darius couldn't remember. Eyes damp from vomiting and now wide with fear, he focused past the open bathroom door to the one beyond the bed. The metal knob turned one way and then in reverse from the grasp of an unknown hand on the other side. A strangulating silence followed as Darius waited for the door to open.

It turned out that he *had* locked it.

Then the shuffle resumed, and whatever was out there moved on.

* * *

The storm lifted. The day brightened. Darius picked himself off the floor, again made aware of the ache in his bones, the hole in his stomach, and a heaviness that seemed to originate from somewhere far deeper than the soul. He made it over to the door and unlocked it. The old door groaned open. In the hallway, a thin trail of dust that hadn't been there before wound across the worn floor. He stared at it without blinking. When it didn't evaporate into the ether, he knelt down and touched the residue with two shaking fingers. What looked like shreds of paper coated his touch— paper that had almost degenerated into nothingness. Standing, he tracked it farther down the hall, around the corner, and to the door to the basement.

Darius set his forehead against the cold, varnished wood.

The basement.

His times down there had been cursory, little more than scouting missions before the purchase. He reached toward the knob but only got halfway before recoiling and walking away.

* * *

The clouds swirled in a misty afternoon sky the color of honey, an after-storm golden gift. Darius pocketed his wallet, set the security alarm, and locked the main door behind him. The post-rain air added a deceptive freshness and mingled well with the fragrance of the green from lawns and hydrangeas. Not so pleasant was the smell in puddles laying stagnant on the pavement or when it mixed with car exhaust.

He ambled down the sidewalk, passing the vacant lot before reaching the bakery. It had closed its doors for the day, but the restaurant attached at the back was open. The Captain's Daughter, which served the freshest Maryland seafood as well as American-Italian fare and comfort classics, was sparsely attended on this night. That suited Darius fine. He caught a note of garlic, Old Bay seasoning, and seafood that was, at first, mouthwatering to experience but like the fresh air, the rush of enjoyment was doomed to pass, and he wondered if he'd be able to stomach anything he ate.

He walked past the restaurant's thick wooden columns in the Doric style and into its tasteful dining room festooned in blue and white checked tablecloths and walls adorned with a revolving gallery of artwork by local painters. Small parties, mostly couples, a few of what he assumed where parents with older children, huddled in private conversations, enjoying catch-of-the-day, bowls of pasta, white wine, and snapshots of normal life at a day's end.

"One for dinner?" the hostess asked.

Darius flashed his theatrical smile. "Yes, only one tonight."

* * *

He chanced the spaghetti and meatballs, his all-time favorite meal, a tall club soda with plenty of ice and a wedge of lemon, and the herb bread instead of garlic. The food was exquisite as expected but filled him after a few bites. He sipped the water, crunched the ice. Whatever pleasure the food offered would soon wane, he knew, leaving his belly filled with imaginary shards of glass.

"Dessert?" his waitress asked.

Darius shook his head. "But I'll take my leftovers home, if you don't mind."

A DREAM WITHIN A DREAM

She picked up the pasta bowl. "You bought the old theater, right?"

"Guilty."

"What are your plans for the place?"

"The Destination has a new destiny," he chuckled at his own private in-joke. "Once she's fixed up and ready, we'll roll out a schedule—starting with a one-man show. But there will be others, you can count on it."

The waitress tsked and shook her head. "I hope it works out better for you than the last owners. I remember when the place closed down. Not a lot of interest in plays or musicals with all that streaming content available and people's faces shoved in their phones."

Darius maintained his smile and thanked her. She returned with his upscale doggy bag. He left a decent tip and joked, "If it doesn't work out, I could always wait tables here, right?"

* * *

The night had attained a musty dampness on his short walk home. *Home.* The Destiny was home now, his townhouse sold for top dollar in the present real estate craze, most of his possessions sold off or donated, his belongings winnowed down to basics or must-have treasures.

The melancholy patter of raindrops falling from eaves and branches played in counterpoint to his footsteps. The Destiny loomed ahead of him, mostly dark, and again, the desolation eroding his insides exerted its dark influence, casting a shroud of sadness around him. *What was I thinking—leaving a high-paying job and excellent medical care for this? All that was familiar and safe for ... a ridiculous dream?*

The rain was over, but his tears were back, unable to be stopped. This was hubris, foolish. Darius' momentum stalled, and he wanted to cry out, vomit his anger like he now so regularly did everything that was and wasn't in his stomach.

He wiped his eyes and ran his fingers through his hair. Why? *Because it isn't too late.* That was the truth he'd sold to himself, the bright spark designed to keep him breathing. It wasn't too late to pursue the dream and passion and inspiration from his younger years.

Darius thought of Tina. Exhumed from behind the mental barriers he'd erected around specific details of his history, he remembered the living room at her father's house, the salads made mostly from canned vegetables they ate doing homework, the plays and discussions about favorite actors.

"I'm going to New York," she said in his memory. "The moment we graduate, that's where I'm headed. I'll land day work on the soaps, work off-Broadway and then on. Build my acting resume. TV and film."

Only that hadn't happened for his best friend, who had given so many passionate speeches following scenes they acted in together from favorite movies, television shows, or improvised from textbooks and, on a few memorable occasions, fortune cookies slips. His favorites had been their recitations of Edgar Allan Poe's poems: *Lenore* and *The Raven*.

Tina had traveled south on a train from New England—the *Independent Traveler*—but had kept going past the city to meet with some lowlife ex-con in the Carolinas. She gave up her dreams for the role as his girlfriend and then his wife. She'd died six years earlier—in his mind not from smoking-related heart disease but boredom.

The theater, so dark. What *was* that thing he'd heard outside the apartment door? What was he thinking in coming here?

"I was thinking that it wasn't too late," Darius whispered. "Not too late to live my oldest, most sacred dream."

Then, resigned to the truth that he had no other choice, he plodded the rest of the way home, aware of the heaviness in his steps and the unpleasant weight in his belly.

* * *

The silence inside the old theater pulsed around him, making sleep difficult. Darius opened the window. No breeze blew. The air grew stagnant. At some untimed point in those restless hours, in a darkness broken only by the telltale dim blinking of his charging phone and tablet, he heard *it* moving around in the shadows of the Destiny.

A DREAM WITHIN A DREAM

It slithered over floors and tested the knobs of closed doors. A scream built in Darius' chest only to die before reaching his throat as he tracked it along the hallway outside his small living space until the unknown horror was directly at the door again. Had he clicked the lock in place? He was sure he had—also that he'd checked it not once but twice. Still, there came that moment of uncertainty when he doubted his own memory.

With the faint creaking of the knob turning came a whispered voice, something damp and infected, as it struggled to draw breath. Darius's nausea returned. He attempted to choke it down. That only worsened his discomfort and forced his eyes to widen until they stung.

He stared. The phlegm-cursed obscenity on the other side of the door shuffled and undulated on, its slithers wet this time, sickening. Darius remained where he was, eyes opened on the darkness, the rest of him engulfed in shadows. Eventually, exhaustion claimed him.

* * *

He slept through the banging on the distant front entrance. His cell phone roused him. Darius woke as he often did now—confused, sick to his stomach, and feeling like his limbs were made of concrete. He grabbed the phone and pulled it from its charging cable on the third ring.

"Hello?"

It was Jones, the cleaning company's foreman. Still clad in the previous day's clothes that now fit like sweat-soaked, shed skin clinging to his flesh, Darius unlocked the sealed apartment door and padded through the silent theater to greet the first of the new Destiny's guests.

* * *

Six bodies in black polo shirts, khakis, and steel-toes set about the task of scrubbing away the filth. Ladders were carried into the theater venue where walls where washed, light bulbs replaced, and seats were steam-cleaned with industrial soap.

Floors were swept and mopped. Carpets and windows were scoured of residue and returned from the dead. By the end of the first long day, much of the Destiny sparkled. The next day cleaners returned for a second pass of the inside while a landscaping crew Darius hired attended to the exterior.

At some point in the chaos of the following week, fresh paint went on—more of the same slate and royal purple combination that worked so well. Darius opted to leave the old marquee up as a nod to the history of the place, but a new sign read: *The Destiny.*

His mood brightened along with the overall appearance of his surroundings. The old popcorn machine and drink dispensers were long gone, but the theater wasn't about refreshments. He decided he'd put a cooler with bottles of water free to any who took in his play. Then, following the performance, goers could enjoy dinner at the Captain's Daughter or other local eateries. Yes, all was looking up!

Until Jones asked him about the basement.

"The basement?" Darius parroted while his brain went blank.

"It's not on our cleaning list, but I remember you saying you wanted it tackled."

Darius nodded. "Have you been down there?"

"It's a mess," Jones said. "Gonna take us another full day just to empty it out. It won't be cheap."

He'd already spent a fortune to get to this point in the theater's Second Act. "Give me until tomorrow to get back to you."

Jones nodded and, with all else met, the cleaning crew packed up ladders, carpet steamers, the rest of their supplies, and departed.

Darius wandered outside. The sweet fragrance of newly mowed lawn drifted through the humidity. The Destiny glowed above him, lit brightly against the evening. He indulged in a smile. The dream was closer to reality.

Whatever doubts he'd suffered lifted. He was fifteen again. Performing in the sophomore class's production of *Grease* with Tina. The year after that, they were both in *The Sound of Music.* Between those plays, they staged their own shows, reading aloud from his grandmother's beat up, beloved hardcover copy of *The Collected Works of Edgar Allan Poe*—one of those must-haves that had traveled with him from that

A DREAM WITHIN A DREAM

other existence to this new life. Every breath drawn in or expelled between performances and for a short time after had been in honor of the actor's craft and life.

It wasn't too late.

He stole another precious minute of happiness, feeling young, before entering the Destiny, locking the front entrance, and switching off the lights.

* * *

The basement. Darius approached. The hallway floors shined from their recent cleaning, all traces of previous dusty tracks gone. The air smelled fresher, of soap and temporary newness. But as he neared the door, the dank atmosphere of the Destiny Theater's underpinnings crept back.

Steeling himself, Darius reached his free hand toward the metal filigree knob and turned. The door croaked open. Beyond, the abyss stretched an unthinkable depth into the center of the Earth.

He switched on the basement lights. Bulbs activated in sequence, dispelling much but not all of the gloom. Darius thumbed on the flashlight in his other hand and headed down the wooden staircase.

Not far past the threshold, the citrus smells and illusion of newness evaporated. Sour air replaced them. Stored in the tomb beneath the theater were a hundred years' worth of detritus, everything from old leftover parts of stage decoration for plays to rusting cans filled with rustier nails, screws, and bolts, and crates containing who-knew-what.

Most of the floor was concrete. Various paths led into even deeper recesses and spaces long unvisited, and in those corners the floors were dirt. A smell of standing water assailed his nose. Darius aimed the flashlight up at the base of the vast wooden ceiling above him, home to a network of pipes. None that he could see leaked.

The melancholy he'd mostly kept ahead of crept closer like a funeral pall. Phantoms surrounded him—stacks of garden trellis from an unknown play left to rot beneath the stage; a wooden horse, not very elegant, perhaps a survivor of *Equus*; trunks containing moldering costumes or props or the souls of an unknown number of the dead, all of whom had dreamed big dreams—stardom, fame, fortune—only to have the Destination Theater as their ending place.

His nausea flared. A foul hiccup raced up Darius' throat and burst across the back of his tongue. He tasted bile and rotten fruit. Sudden lightheadedness nearly overwhelmed him. He made it over to a wooden chair among the relics in the tomb of dead dreams beneath the stage and sat. Holding his breath, he choked down the foulness painted onto his taste buds. The discomfort passed enough for him to draw in a metered sip of air—and to notice something *other* thanks to the shaking beam of light aimed at the floor.

Beside Darius' left sneaker, another of those trails made of what looked to be shredded paper and dust formed a pattern across the concrete. He wiped his mouth, willed his shaking hand to steady, and traced the flashlight's beam along the tracks. The imprint led around piles of stage rigging and an ancient wardrobe. Darius ordered his legs to move and approached the dark realm as yet hidden from view.

The thing he'd heard moving around in the theater at night and, sometimes, in daylight hours—he'd blamed it on the medicine and then his own body, which had betrayed him. The worm was chewing its way through memories and reality as well as membranes and muscle, leaving him in a landscape haunted by dark hallucinations.

On the final creep around the old wardrobe, however, Darius questioned the thing in the hallways as a figment. A will o'the wisp didn't leave tracks. These led to the remains of a big cardboard box that had either been crushed under weight or exploded from within. Shreds of paper layered the surrounding patch of dirt floor. As he neared, Darius caught the bitter, yellow smell of rodents. No, this was worse than that.

A *nest*, his inner voice warned.

He aimed the flashlight's beam into the gutted carton. Inside was more paper, most of it no larger than confetti. Darius poked at the edges with the flashlight. A corner of a thin, printed book appeared. The nest was made from the remains of old playbills.

A DREAM WITHIN A DREAM

How long he stood and stared, Darius couldn't fathom. The unpleasant contrasts of boiling and freezing under his skin returned. At some untimed point, so did the slither-scrape of the obscenity that had built the nest. Darius unstuck from his palsy and raised the flashlight. Past the nest were more pieces of things, all stacked around a channel leading over dirt floor and into the shadows directly beneath the theater's stage.

Movement—he only saw it in the splintered second it took for the revulsion to claw up from his stomach. In the unsteady beam's flickers a head appeared, featureless apart from its inflamed red color, the size of a man but bent in an undulating version of a slug's crawl ... no, a *worm's* ... pushing forward, pulsating, *writhing*. In that hideous and unforgettable moment imprinted forever upon his consciousness, Darius saw part of its body alter as it charged from the bowels chewed beneath the theater directly at him.

It became almost human.

He jumped back, turned, and raced in the direction of the staircase. Audible over his own strangled breaths and the throb of the entombed space around him were its rapid, dusty slithers playing in counterpoint to its phlegm-choked growls. Darius reached the stairs. The horror extended its head and chased him up. Somehow, the flashlight was still in his grip. He swung and focused all of his effort into the strike. The head of the flashlight struck its target hard enough to shatter the bulb in its case. The sickening thing just attaching to his ankle let go.

Sobbing, he kicked and jumped up and didn't stop again until he was behind the locked door of the little apartment at the rear of the Destiny Theater.

* * *

He wept, unable to catch his breath. *What was that thing?* The question repeated over and over, playing on a loop inside his thoughts.

Outside, the day continued as though it were unremarkable. The sun's light beamed down. A humid breeze stirred the threadbare curtains at the one open window. Traffic sounded. A bird cried out. All were elements of a sane world.

His aches caught up to him, and Darius slid down to the floor, wondering if he'd be able to pick himself back up to standing once the exhaustion passed. He braced against the varnished wood with his spine and listened for it. Nothing. The Destiny sat under a deceptive stillness.

A dream, surely. A *nightmare*—one born of medicines and metastasis; not monsters that haunted basements. Until he peered down at his foot and saw his sneaker chewed at the heel and a trickle of fresh blood.

* * *

His heart rate slowed and Darius stood. Outside, the world had turned dark, and he ached all over. He checked the lock on the door again and crooked his ear up at the transom. Nothing.

The thing in the basement ... he'd found its nest, its home. The horror had prowled around the empty theater almost from the moment he'd landed. Had he disturbed it by moving about overhead? Or had he somehow awakened it from its version of hibernation? For a moment, it had almost looked human.

This was his place now, *his* domain.

He washed and ignored his fresh bruises, changed clothes, and unlocked the door.

* * *

At the restaurant, he sat alone at a table for two and pretended to peruse the menu. On this night, a waiter he guessed was in his twenties brought him water with a wedge of lemon and the basket of bread rolls baked on the premises.

"What can I get you tonight?" the young man asked.

Darius wondered if his smile was convincing. "A steak—the thickest one you've got."

It soon appeared, grilled medium as instructed, crusted on the outside to perfection and making what remained of his appetite water. There was a big, sharp knife perfect for cutting meat on the side of the platter. He ate a few bites of it, plus

A DREAM WITHIN A DREAM

one forkful each of cauliflower hash and roasted parsnips, then asked for a doggy bag. Darius made sure to leave an extra tip.

* * *

The Destiny brooded beneath a mix of silence and anticipation. Shadows and sadness closing in.

As he always did, Darius knelt before the back row of seats in a show of respect before walking to the front. He took the chair at center. The candelabra lights, their dead bulbs replaced, radiated a golden glow down on the stage and its surroundings.

Why? Why did I wait so long to live rather than exist?

He drank in the beauty of that stage, so long silent, and the strange magic contained within the elegant walls with their ribbons of wedding cake molding.

He'd made a lot of money over the years but little more. His next breath clotted halfway down his throat. It would have been better to starve if suffering was in service of art, of happiness. His consciousness returned to that grave, to the roses, and more, to the one they were left in memory of. All those private recitals of Poe's poetry ...

"You would have understood," he whispered to the stillness. "You, who fought your own demons over that which burned so passionately within you. Maybe our demons are one and the same."

The Destiny maintained its glint along with the illusion of newness and hope for several tense seconds longer before the sound reached him—that undulating slither of something writhing, writhing, writhing.

Closer.

He heard it moving among the seats.

"Do you know who I am?" it asked in a juicy, alien voice neither fully male nor female.

Darius froze.

"All the tears ever spilled on that stage," it continued. "Every dead inspiration and wasted prayer ... the residue of extinguished passion that seeped and oozed between the cracks in the floorboards to pool beneath the performers. That's who I am. I feast on dreams and the angels who lurk unseen in the audience!"

It slithered into view, into the light—a giant red, writhing worm. The worm stared at him through eyes not there and sniffed the air through its lack of a nose; limbless, the length of a man, its red, red hide coated in the confetti of shredded playbills.

"And I am inside you now, devouring those eight-pointed stars of inspiration along with the rest of your organs!"

Darius focused and thawed. He reached down, drew the meat knife from concealment in his sneaker and pant leg and, gripping the handle, in one fluid motion threw himself at the hideous thing in front of him. He drove the sharp point into its head—deep. The abomination recoiled and screamed in a phlegm-soaked ghoulish register. The worm flailed back. Darius got off another strike, this cut even deeper, longer. Red gushed into the air. The worm, its shrieks now deafening within the cavernous space of the theater's heart, spilled back, writhing, and undulated up the five stairs to the stage.

A foul smell of spoiled fruit filled Darius' next desperate gulping breath. Going on automatic in a kind of actor's trance, he marched up the steps, weapon in hand. As he neared to deliver the killing blow, the obscenity altered its shape, becoming something—*someone*—far worse.

Four limbs and a head sprouted out of its blooded and kicking mass.

"No, Darius, *please!*" Tina begged.

Darius recoiled from the nude woman's body with his dead best friend's face. He froze. The body mewled. And then it laughed. Darius squeezed on the knife's handle. As he resumed his march toward it, the thing on the stage blew apart in a cascade of red, red blood. That blood seeped through the cracks, atoms, and molecules of the Destiny, there in a horrific splatter one instant and completely gone the next.

A terrible silence followed.

And then Darius screamed.

* * *

A DREAM WITHIN A DREAM

He called the local newspapers. He made signs and hung them around town and in the Destiny's now-clean windows. He lit the marquee, unlocked and opened the doors dressed in an audacious satin blazer, jeans, and a T-shirt bearing the likeness of Edgar Allan Poe. Darius waited. Free water. Free admission. Free entertainment—the play was the thing.

ACTOR, ACTOR, the signs read. *The often funny but ultimately tragic tale of a man named Darius—7 p.m. at the new Destiny Theater.*

At 6:57, Darius tipped a look past the curtains to see the seats were all empty.

Five minutes later, nothing had changed, and no one was there.

"*Dead inspiration,*" he whispered.

He wanted to cry, to add his tears to those already wept in sacrament to the gods of the stage. The worm turned inside him. He felt it erode flesh and something else—soul.

Close the theater. Switch off the lights. Give up.

He marched down the five steps, aware of the invisible burden pressing upon his shoulders. It was the end. The dream had died.

Darius took another step and then stopped. Expelling a cleansing breath, he turned and marched back up the five steps and onto the stage. He shook the tension out of his body, closed his eyes, and bowed.

"It was all an act," he said, projecting his voice at its most commanding. "From the time I came into this world, I wanted to be someone else. Oh, I had a nice delivery, mind you, and my parents were okay ..." He smiled, waited for the laughs he expected but were absent. "I just liked being a chameleon, wearing other identities, *acting.*"

Eyes closed, he regaled the empty velvet seats with stories of running down the road with an apple green towel tied around his neck and pretending to be a superhero—Granny Smith Apple Man!—and of loving Halloween because it meant dressing up and playing roles. Of not being able to sleep during naptime in kindergarten because they were rehearsing for a play. Of the fieldtrip in first grade and the luscious strawberry ice cream at the place next door to where they performed summer stock. Of TV shows and movies and the thousand genius actors who'd inspired him. Of Tina and high school plays and especially those wonderful, private readings of Poe. Of a corporate life and cancer and a kind of coming home.

"To my *destiny*," he said, and, eyes still shut, Darius bowed.

Applause sounded, shocking in its intensity. His eyes shot open and he straightened, at first convinced that what he saw was more madness, more side effects of the rot feasting upon his insides.

The audience was filled to capacity—every seat!

Darius' shock passed enough for him to recognize those in attendance—the great Martin Landau, Barry Morse, Zienia Merton, Tony Anholt, and Suzanne Roquette. Gene Kelly, Gene Tierney, Dana Andrews, Jimmy Stewart, Dean Martin, and Clifton Webb. Boris Karloff and Bela Lugosi. Lorne Greene and Richard Hatch. Darren McGavin and Simon Oakland. Jonathan Frid, Ted Cassidy, and Christopher George. Jonathan Harris and Guy Williams. Funnymen who'd made him laugh until he'd cried—Benny Hill, Benny Ruben, the three Howard Brothers, Larry Fine, and Joe Besser among them. Bogart and Bacall. Basehart and Hedison. Larry Hagman and Barbara Bel Geddes. Patricia Barry, Phil Carey, Clint Ritchie, David Canary, and a hundred others. And Tina, front row, to the right of center.

And at that very center seat, front row, sat Edgar Allan Poe, the greatest of all writers in Darius' estimation.

The legends all stood and the applause continued. Nodding in understanding, Darius bowed, aware that he no longer ached anywhere because he was filled only with light. He had released all the rest and was completely healed by his passion.

"And now that final curtain call," he said as the lights dimmed and he walked off stage to join all who'd gone before him. "The one when Death applauds us all."

About the Author

Raised on a healthy diet of creature double features and classic SF TV, Gregory L. Norris writes regularly for numerous short story anthologies, national magazines, novels, and the occasional episode for TV or film. Gregory novelized the NBC Made-for-TV classic by Gerry Anderson, *The Day After Tomorrow: Into Infinity* (as well as a sequel and a forthcoming third entry into the franchise for Anderson Entertainment in the U.K.), a movie he watched as an eleven-year-old sitting cross-legged on the living room floor of the enchanted cottage where he grew up. Gregory won HM in the 2016 Roswell Awards in Short SF Writing and was a 2022 Finalist. He once worked as a screenwriter on two episodes of Paramount's *Star Trek: Voyager*. Kate Mulgrew, *Voyager's* "Captain Janeway," blurbed his book of short stories and novellas, *The Fierce and Unforgiving Muse*, stating, "In my seven years on *Voyager*, I don't think I've met a writer more capable of writing such a book—and writing it so beautifully."

In late 2019, Gregory sold an option on his modern Noir feature film screenplay, *Amandine*, to the new Hollywood production company Snarkhunter LLC, owned by actor Dan Lench, a devotee of Gregory's writing. In late 2020, Snarkhunter optioned Gregory's tetralogy Horror film based upon four of his short stories, *Ride Along*. Twice Norris has been nominated for the Pushcart Prize. He is the author of the novel *Ex Marks the Spot* (Woodhall Press) and the forthcoming release of SF tales of wonder and adventure stretching from Sol to Pluto, *The Solar System* (September 2022), and a delightfully dark dystopian novel, *The Lost City of Books*.

Gregory lives and writes at Xanadu, a century-old house perched on a hill in New Hampshire's North Country with spectacular mountain views, with his rescue cat and emerald-eyed muse. Follow his literary adventures at: www.gregorylnorris.blogspot.com.

Love Books?

SUPPORT AUTHORS – buy directly from independent publishers. This puts more royalty dollars into the pockets of your favorite author – and gives them time to write their next book.

Visit us for links to our other books as well as many other vibrant publishing companies to find the book for you.

Send a note to join our **Book Launch List.**

Director@vanvelzerpress.com

These ARE The Books You've Been Looking For.

Vanvelzerpress.com